USA TODAY BESTSELLING AUTHOR

Dale Mayer

HEROES FOR HIRE

RORY'S ROSE: HEROES FOR HIRE, BOOK 13
Beverly Dale Mayer
Valley Publishing Ltd.

ISBN-13: 978-1-773360-63-8
Print Edition

Books in This Series:

Carson's Choice: Heroes for Hire, Book 28

Dante's Decision: Heroes for Hire, Book 29

Steven's Solace: Heroes for Hire, Book 30

Boxed Sets and Bundles

https://geni.us/Bundlepage

About This Book

Reconnect with unforgettable secondary characters from SEALs of Honor in a brand-new spin-off series. Previously Levi and his team were caught unaware by a cartel in Mexico and suffered the consequences of betrayal. That event drove Levi to establish his own company, Legendary Securities, on property inherited from a reclusive uncle. In the pursuit of life, liberty and the pursuit of happiness, he employs former SEALs he trusts implicitly to work with him on dangerous, covert private missions.

Book 13: Rory's Rose

Rory is an animal lover. In his mind, any veterinarian who does as much pro bono work as Louise, the local vet, deserves his help when she gets into trouble…

Louise works long hours at her own veterinarian clinic. When she receives an unexpected delivery one day, complete with a dead deliveryman, a domino-series of events puts her and her clinic full of precious animals in danger.

Rory is the first to volunteer to keep her safe. Professional reasons quickly become personal. Louise is everything he's ever wanted and never expected to find in a single woman. He's looking forward to a future together, and the only way to ensure that is to stop whatever's endangering her and her animals.

Unfortunately, the killer isn't leaving a witness to his

crimes. At first, Rory and the team at Legendary Securities make headway in discovering what's going on, but the tables turn in an instant and, for the first time since he joined the team, Rory's vision of a satisfactory resolution—and happily-ever-after—may not be in the cards.

Sign up to be notified of all Dale's releases here!
https://geni.us/DaleNews

Prologue

AS HE DROVE toward the property, Rory Bellamy knew he should have told Jace and Tyson outright he wasn't interested. Nothing about the look of the massive cement compound, rising in the darkness of night before him, could make him feel this was *his* place, not even temporarily.

It wasn't the most welcoming sight he'd ever seen. Nothing like the family ranch.

But was that important at this stage of his life? Besides, it wasn't like he wanted a ranch for himself. So that whole scenario—while great to step back into his roots a bit to help out—wasn't his future.

Hell yeah, like the other men in his unit, he'd been lost this last year. Maybe more lost than they'd been. Michael had his own place where he'd holed up, and Jace had come to the ranch to help Rory's family for a few months. Rory greatly appreciated it, considering he had kept the family ranch afloat while his brother recovered from a bad tractor accident.

Rory would have gone to the ranch sooner if he'd known he was needed. But, damn it, how was he supposed to know if no one said anything? He didn't live in Texas anymore. He'd stuck to California, even after leaving the military. Mostly because he didn't know where else to go. Having a reason to come home made it seem less like an excuse and more like a purpose.

How could he tell his father and brother how lost he'd been? That he wanted—no—needed to return to his roots? That line of conversation would bring up a mess of questions he had no intention of answering.

Thankfully his father *had* called and told him what happened. Rory had flown home immediately to help until Dennis was back on his feet. Rory had intended to be there for only a few months but had ended up staying almost nine. He'd enjoyed those months, and then it was time to go.

His brother was strong enough to take over again. The ranch had the boss back, and Rory was an unpaid ranch hand, getting in the way and struggling to let go of the reins and to return control to Dennis.

After one particular argument, he realized the problem was him. This wasn't his place. He was always welcome to visit, but it wasn't his home.

He didn't have one.

The sense of being lost returned in a vicious wave.

He turned off the engine and stepped from his battered pickup truck. He tilted his beat-up cowboy hat off his forehead and looked at the imposing structure. The longer he looked at it, the better he felt. It was massive, ugly and cold-looking, but it had timelessness to it. It was solid. It had been built to withstand the world, the elements, time and anything Mother Nature could throw at it. It no longer looked ugly as much as it looked immovable. A certain comfort existed in that.

But he had to remember it wasn't his home either. Michael might have bought the property bordering it, but that was Michael. Not Rory. Michael had put down roots.

Rory was afraid he didn't have any to put down.

A nearby door opened suddenly, and he could see shadows as several people walked out. A security lamp turned on, highlighting the men standing in front of him.

Jace, Tyson, Michael. Easy men to identify. So many more stood beside them. And women …

Suddenly shy, he tipped his hat and in a husky drawl said, "Good evening."

"About time you got here," Jace said, stepping forward to slap him on the shoulder. "I was hoping you'd make it. How's Dennis doing?"

"He's back on top, so I figured maybe you guys could use a hand." Rory stepped forward, only now seeing Ice and Levi.

Ice's face lit up. "Rory?" She raced toward him and threw her arms around him. "I'm so happy to see you. Levi told me that he'd offered you a job, but he didn't say you'd accepted."

"I didn't. I just arrived," he apologized and dropped his arms from Ice, smiling at her. Ice had adopted him into her friend group a long time ago. He studied her face. "This suits you."

She beamed. "It does indeed." Her gaze was intense, searching, and she wouldn't let him evade her focus. Ever since she'd heloed in and picked him up, badly injured from a mission gone wrong, she'd kept an eye on him. She'd dragged him out for a few beers with her friends time and time again.

Levi stepped forward and shook Rory's hand with a grin on his face. "About time you got here."

Some of Rory's initial uneasiness dropped away.

Ice turned to look at Levi. "You didn't tell me he was coming."

"I didn't know when he'd get here. I just told him the door was always open. I figured he'd find his way eventually."

Ice's smile was so damn beautiful as she stared at Levi that Rory suddenly wished someone was in his life who looked at him the same way. But he needed to get his own shit together first.

Levi swung his arm toward the doorway. "You've got a lot of friends here. Welcome home."

The wording stopped Rory for a long moment. How did Levi realize exactly what Rory was missing? A sense of home and someone in it to share his life with.

Then a series of odd yips filled the air. He glanced down to see a fat puppy barely walking with several siblings behind it, all waddling toward the group.

"Sorry," a tall brunette woman said. "They've had their bottle, and now they need to go to the bathroom, so I brought them outside. I didn't realize you were all out here."

"No problem. Louise, come meet Rory, the newest member of the team," Ice said.

Rory squatted down as one of the puppies struggled to make it to him, its nose quickly pushing into Rory's hand. He chuckled and scooped up the pudge. "What's this guy's name?"

"We're trying to come up with some," Levi said. "These guys are from Anna and Flynn's place. The mother has no milk, and Anna needed help feeding them, so we're fostering them until Anna can find homes."

Louise laughed. "Good luck with that." She smiled at Rory and reached out to shake his hand. "I'm a vet. I came to check out these little guys." She walked to her car as she said, "I can see they are all well looked after. I'll come back in a few days."

Rory, his arms full of adorableness, watched her drive away. When he turned to the others, he found a speculative look on Ice's face. He raised an eyebrow. "What's the matter?"

Jace snorted and said, "Don't worry about it. Give in now. It'll happen no matter what you do, so surrender to it from the start. It's easier that way."

Rory stared at him in confusion.

Levi grinned. "Come on inside. Looks like you'll fit right in."

Chapter 1

W EEKS LATER RORY walked back into the compound, surprised at how easily he had fit in. He had a duffel bag over his shoulder and a second travel bag in his hand, his trusty hat perched on his head. He'd been looking forward to getting back since he left. Some jobs were like that. And it had taken way less time than he'd expected to look at the compound as *his* place. Everyone had been open, friendly. Accepting. After an initial few days of wandering the compound, he'd been put to work with a vengeance. And he'd loved every minute of it.

He'd been part of a dozen jobs since he'd arrived. He loved the diversity, the change of pace, and, most of all, he loved being busy. It had helped put his time on the ranch in perspective.

Somehow in the last few weeks he'd found another calling, showing him once again the adaptability of the human spirit. Thankfully …

Still, he looked forward to walking inside and seeing the puppies. One in particular. That dratted puppy had found the hole in his heart and had filled it with her saggy jowls and her face washes with her huge tongue and her loving acceptance. He'd named her Rose without realizing it.

She was just too incredibly sweet to be believed. She still slept with her mom, and, so far, Alfred, Levi and Ice had managed to keep the puppies on the main floor and not up in the bedrooms on the second and third floors. But he wondered how long it would be before that changed.

They were trying to avoid having all six adopted away from the compound. Anna, who ran the rescue center around the corner and had brought the puppies here, had been by a couple times, and Rory had had a chance to meet her. So many people were in this compound—it was not only a family, it was an extended family. He likened this group to the big Italian and Greek families. Except all the members of this family were relatively the same age, which made it a unique experience.

They could set up their own baseball team or soccer team or football team. Considering a recreational spot in the backyard had been mapped out as part of the new development, Rory wondered if they should form a water polo team. He loved water sports himself. Ice and Levi were putting in tennis courts and a swimming pool, plus a hot tub and a field for a good scrimmage. He laughed at the term. Maybe it had more to do with the thought of taking Rose out there. He had to stop thinking in terms of her being here permanently.

He knew she would be adopted. She was too adorable not to be. He walked into the kitchen area and smiled. Alfred caught sight of him just as he set a big platter of muffins on the table. With a scolding finger, Alfred said, "Don't touch."

"Oh, you're a cruel man, Alfred," Rory said with a smile. He glanced around. "If nobody needs me right now, I'll head upstairs and grab a shower."

"Good idea. Coffee and muffins in thirty minutes."

"I'll be back." He walked through the kitchen to the big

hallway leading to the elevator but stopped and turned to look at Alfred. "How are the puppies?"

Alfred's face beamed. "They're doing great. And, yes, Rose is wonderful."

"I'm sure she is," he said with a smile. "I know I shouldn't get too attached, but it's pretty hard not to."

Alfred nodded. "I'm feeling that way myself."

"Any word from Anna as to their futures?"

"Not yet. But she's done pretty well adopting out most of the animals that come through her place."

"I know. Sadly, I know."

Refusing to look in on them yet, Rory picked up his bags and headed to his room. Once there he stripped down to his skin and stepped into a hot shower. By the time he was cleaned, shampooed, shaven and dressed again, he'd used up all of his thirty minutes before breakfast. He looked at his dirty laundry and shrugged. It would wait until later. He stepped outside his room and saw several women who lived in the place walking down the hall. They stopped and smiled at him.

"Are you back in Houston for now?" Sienna asked.

He nodded. "I think so."

"Have you seen the puppies since you got back?" Katrina asked.

"Not yet. I'm just about to head there," he admitted with a sideways grin. "It'll be hard to let them—Rose in particular—go."

"I know. We're working on Ice and Levi to let us keep two."

"Like anybody can agree which two," he scoffed. Inside, he had to admit it was a hell of a good idea—as long as Rose was one of them. "If you convince Alfred that he needs them, you know they would give in then. He's the one who looks after them the most anyway."

"Not to mention they'd be good company for him."

"Right, like he's alone at any point," Merk said, joining them. He smacked Rory on the shoulder. "You're getting all the easy jobs lately."

"I am," Rory said. "Not a bad way to get my feet wet though, I suppose."

"This is small stuff," Sienna said. "He'll get hit with some of the tougher ones. I know a lot of different jobs are coming across our desk right now. Not exactly sure what's happening, but I suspect people will be leaving today or tomorrow."

Merk looked at her with interest. "Anything I might want to snag?"

"It's not like you get your choice," she said gently.

Merk just gave her that grin. Rory knew Merk *did* get his choice. That was the benefit of having been here since the beginning. Merk, Stone, Rhodes and Levi. They *were* Legendary Security. By now Levi and Ice had to have at least sixteen to eighteen men working for them. Every one of them had a life partner—except Rory. That really sucked. But, if his partner could be little fluffy Rose, he'd be good.

Instead of taking the elevator, they all walked down the big wide staircase and arrived on the main floor together as a boisterous happy group. That was what Rory liked. As they all walked into the dining room, the puppies came out from the kitchen. Instantly they were picked up and cuddled. Their little yelps filled the room.

Levi walked in, straight to the coffeepot, poured himself a cup before looking at Rory. "It was a really bad idea to foster these guys, wasn't it?" he asked.

Sienna chuckled. "Not necessarily. Everybody needs love."

"Uh-huh," Levi said. "We aren't keeping them," he warned.

Ice walked in. Seeing Levi with a cup of coffee, she poured herself one too. She had barely put it on the table before she opened her arms and one of the puppies was handed to her. She cuddled it close and scratched its chin and around its eyes. The puppy obligingly licked her face and every other body part it could reach. With a wink to the other ladies, she dropped the puppy into Levi's arms. "Don't be such a grouch," she said. "Love a puppy."

She took the mug from his hand so he didn't spill it and turned her back on him just so he could spend a few minutes with the puppy. Rory watched and laughed. Ice knew exactly how this worked. Rory pulled up a chair, sat down and put Rose on the floor. She wandered off, looking for something to chew. Lately it had been somebody's shoe underneath the table. No matter where they sat, the puppies looked for footwear to chomp on. Ice handed Rory a cup of coffee. He looked at it with surprise. "Thanks."

Bailey entered with two platters of muffins. She looked flushed from the heat of the stove. Rory glanced over at her and smiled. "Thank you."

She laughed. "You haven't even tried them yet. Maybe they're awful."

"I haven't eaten anything from you and Alfred that wasn't wonderful."

She smiled.

Dakota joined her. He snagged a muffin off the tray in her hands, kissed her on the temple and said, "Thanks, sweetie."

She rolled her eyes at him and handed the tray around. "They are not just for you."

When a vehicle drove up, Stone's voice was heard over the PA. "The vet's here."

That just added to the excitement. When Louise walked in, Rose waddled over to greet her. Louise picked up the pudgy puppy, chuckled, gave her a good scratch and said, "I figured if you were too close to Alfred, that you'd gain weight very quickly."

As it happened, Alfred walked in with a platter of some fancy Danishes.

Rory laughed because it seemed such an appropriate time for her to complain about Alfred's rather wonderful cooking.

"Am I interrupting something?" Louise frowned.

Ice walked over with a big smile and a puppy and said, "Absolutely not. We're just having coffee. Will you join us?"

"I'd love to." Louise sat down and asked Alfred, "Any problems with the puppies?"

With a proud fatherly smile he shook his head. "They're doing just lovely."

"I can see that." Louise checked over the puppy in her arms while Ice retrieved a cup of coffee for her. "This one looks healthy." She handed her off to Rory and said, "You're still here, are you?"

Rory laughed as he juggled the furry ball of love in his arms. "Yeah. I'm adjusting."

"This place is a zoo," she said with a laugh. "But it looks like you've settled in fine."

"I'm adapting." He chuckled and hugged Rose. Maybe the excitement got to her, or maybe she hadn't had enough sleep, but she'd given up squirming to curl into the crook of his neck and fall asleep. He just held her close.

The vet gave him a knowing look.

He nodded. "I know. It'll be painful to let her go." He cuddled her close, not ready to put her in her bed with her siblings.

Drinking his coffee, enjoying being at the compound, he settled back. The conversation shifted from animals to security before shifting lightning fast to muffins, pool engineering and back to renovations. He loved that here. Myriad topics were always covered on the go. Immense brainpower was housed here, and intelligent debate was everywhere. He loved the stimulation and openness. Only after the coffee did Rory realize something was bothering Louise. As soon as the idea caught hold, he studied her carefully, noting the pinched look on her face, the tense grip on her cup of coffee. He didn't know her well, but she seemed ill at ease. As if she wanted to say something but didn't feel she should.

"Is this just an animal visit, or is something else behind it?" he asked in a low voice.

She glanced at him and then quickly away.

"A lot of people are here with a lot of skill sets, if you need help." He leaned in closer. "And it's confidential."

SILENCE FELL IN the room as others tuned in. Louise looked around nervously, yet she only saw curiosity and acceptance. She settled into her skin somewhat. She hadn't planned to talk about this, but, having seen this place, knowing the people, there was just something secure and dependable about them.

"I don't even know what I need." She winced because

that would only bring on more questions. "It's probably a matter for the authorities anyway."

Ice was seated on the other side of the table. She leaned over and asked, "What's a matter for the authorities?"

"I think somebody is mixing up the wrong drugs for animals."

Silence returned as everyone stared. "What do you mean?" Levi asked, his voice stern.

Louise took a deep breath. "I got a shipment of drugs from my usual supplier but with different labels on them. When I asked the driver about it, he couldn't give me a decent explanation. He hurriedly grabbed the case from my arms and reloaded it on the truck. He apologized, saying it was a wrong shipment. Then he was gone damn fast."

It was probably a mistake to bring it up, but she couldn't let it go in her head. At least Levi's team would let her know if she was making something out of nothing. "The thing is, he left one of the cases behind. I tracked it back to the company and called them. They said they didn't know anything about it. How it was obviously a mistake. I took a closer look. The medicine looked to be in the company's packaging. As if somebody had opened the packages, dumped the contents of the bottles, filled them with something else, then resealed them."

"Is that possible?" Ice asked.

"I never thought about it until I ended up with this case. So I'd have said no before, and now I feel like I need to say ... maybe," she admitted.

"What made you think the wrong drugs were inside the containers?"

Rory's tone was calm, without making it sound like she was making this up. She appreciated that. As such it was easy to answer. "I used to sell a lot of veterinarian supplies. So I do know the company's products. Plus I use them for my own work. The one I opened had a different texture to the powder. I checked with the company, and they confirmed they haven't changed their formula. I don't know if it was my imagination, but I don't want to use the drugs, just in case, and now I can't get it out of my mind."

"Do you still have them?"

Louise nodded. "Yes."

Silence once again fell in the big dining room. Even Alfred, who just arrived, froze midstep with a tray of something else delicious looking in his hands.

Louise looked around the room and asked, "Why?"

"Several reasons. First, if something is wrong," Levi said, "we want to make sure the drugs aren't administered to animals. What color is the substance inside the bottles?"

"That's part of the problem. When I looked at it, my mind immediately thought of something else. Because it was white."

"As in cocaine? Heroin?" Levi leaned forward, studying her face intently.

"I don't know the difference," she admitted. "I'm not sure about anything. For all I know, it was my imagination. Like, when you notice someone who looks at you in a shifty way, as if they're nervous, and they just want to get away. As if they realize they've made a mistake, and it's a big one, and they quickly grab and run?" She shook her head. "The delivery man didn't waste any time leaving the parking lot."

"What kind of vehicle was he driving?"

"An old delivery truck. I don't remember what was printed on the side of the truck, but it was one of the standard brown trucks we see everywhere. I didn't look that closely," she admitted. "Why would I? And when? After he took off, I couldn't see anything on the back panel of the vehicle."

"So, like a pickup truck, a delivery truck or a big semi-truck?" Rory asked beside her.

"One of those smaller panel delivery trucks. But it wasn't as big as what I've seen before." She frowned, then she shrugged. "I really don't have any way to measure it. I just gave it a passing glance."

"But you couldn't see the license plate when he took off?" Rory asked.

"I didn't look. I'm not sure if it was even there. The truck was pretty muddy."

"Do you have security at the clinic?" Ice asked.

Louise turned to look at her in surprise. "Yes. I do. I haven't checked the feed to see if the truck shows up there or not."

"Somebody will go back with you. He can take a look, run through the camera feed and look for any sign of a license plate or what kind of truck it was and possibly catch the driver's face."

"As for a description, all I can really say is he was Hispanic-looking and dressed in black jeans and a gray T-shirt. I don't think he spoke English very well."

"So, no uniform?"

She stared at Rory in surprise. "Actually no. He didn't have on a uniform."

The others nodded.

"You really think they're smuggling drugs? Why deliver them to a vet clinic then?"

"They could also be making regular deliveries, and the shipments got mixed up."

They asked her dozens more questions, but she was hard-pressed to answer any of them. Finally she stood and said, "I have to get back. I've stayed longer than I intended to."

Rory glanced over at Levi and raised an eyebrow.

Levi nodded. "Rory will follow you back. Give him access to your security feed, and let's see if he can find anything."

She hesitated. "Do you really think it's something serious?"

He gave her a flat stare. "If it is, and you don't do something about it, it could be bad."

"In what way?" she protested. "I didn't have anything to do with it."

"No, but that is the second issue we didn't discuss. If one case of the product was left behind, is that driver or his boss coming back after it? If it's drugs, like cocaine or heroin, it'll have a high street value. Whoever is moving these drugs will want them back. They'll retrieve them no matter what they have to do."

She could do nothing but stare at him. She hadn't once considered that.

"In other words," Rory added quietly, "your life is in danger until this is settled."

Chapter 2

L OUISE WAS STILL numb by the time she got into her small truck. She pulled out slowly from the compound and onto the main road. Rory was in another truck behind her. She could see the cowboy hat perched on his head. She didn't know what to think. It was just unbelievable to consider it was illegal drugs. However, the more she thought about it, that *had* been her instinctive reaction. The driver's movements and attitude had just been too nervous. As if he was doing something wrong. She honked the horn, as they all did, as she passed Anna's place. Louise was due to stop in there in the next couple of days. Right now she needed to return to the clinic and make sure everything was okay. It was only a ten-minute drive, but it seemed like forever.

She walked into the front office and smiled at everyone to let them know she was here. She had another vet working at the clinic. Thankfully he was in and working his way through the steady stream of patients. With Rory at her side, she headed to the rear of the clinic. It took her a moment to find the case of product, as she'd tucked it in the back with a sign not to open it. She pulled it down and showed it to him. "This is it."

She watched as he studied it carefully. "It looks professionally produced," he announced. "Was the packaging still all around the bottles before you cut it open at the corner?"

"Yes, I just cut the corner so I could get out the one bottle. It *was* very professional looking." She nodded. "They are fair-size bottles though. Too big actually. That's one of the things that made me suspicious."

"What size would you expect these to be?"

"About one-third of that size."

He nodded. "Show me the video camera feed."

She led the way through to the office and brought up the cameras. He quickly ran through the security feed back to the time she had mentioned and watched as the delivery truck driver came into view. It was a simple exchange, but even Rory could see how nervous the driver was. "Well, he certainly takes off fast," Rory said.

"I know, right?"

"Can I print some of these pictures?"

"Sure. Whatever you need." She walked to the door. "Do you need me for anything?"

He glanced at her in surprise, then at the full waiting room and shook his head. "Go. You're needed in the clinic now."

With a smile, she entered the waiting room, picked up the top file off the counter and started on her schedule. She did a lot of fieldwork and was often gone, but she always tried to get back in time to at least take some of the stress off Jimmy. He'd been working with her for close to a year now. He was help she desperately needed. The place was a beehive of animals. She loved her job, and the last thing she wanted was to have any dangerous drugs in circulation that could harm her animals.

A few hours later, Nancy, her receptionist, walked into Louise's office with a stack of folders as Louise returned after her last patient of the morning. "Okay, you get an hour's break. Almost," Nancy said with a cheerful smile as she dropped the stack on the corner of Louise's desk. "No more patients for at least forty minutes."

Louise sat down with a sigh and rubbed her temple. "Now that's good to hear."

The receptionist walked off, then turned at the doorway and said, "Your boyfriend left a long time ago. He had a note for you. Let me go get it."

Startled, Louise wondered who the hell Nancy was talking about. Louise didn't have a boyfriend. Hadn't had a boyfriend since she started the clinic five years ago. Who had time for that? When she'd hired Jimmy, she'd briefly wondered if he might be boyfriend material and quickly found out he *was* boyfriend material but already had a boyfriend himself. She chuckled at that. The two of them were good together. She, on the other hand, was alone, and she'd been alone for a long time now.

Nancy returned and held out a small piece of paper. "You may not play around much, Doc," she teased, "but when you pick one, you really pick a good one."

Louise looked up from the note as she unfolded it and frowned. "I don't even know who you're talking about."

"Rory."

"Oh." Louise could feel the heat rising up her neck. "He is cute, isn't he?"

"*Cute* isn't the word I'd use. He's adorable. That smile of his, well, that's quite a heartbreaker there." Nancy hesitated and then said, "Is there something between the two of you?"

Hearing an odd tone in Nancy's voice, Louise lifted her head and looked at her longtime friend and assistant. "Why?"

Nancy grinned with impudence. "Because, if you aren't

interested, I might be."

"No," Louise responded a little too sharply for her liking.

Nancy took off, laughing.

Louise just sat there and stared at the doorway. Rory was a nice guy, but why had she been so strong to deny her interest? Trying to refocus, she stared down at the note. It was short and to the point.

Louise, I've printed out several images from the security feed, and I've taken photographs of the case of product. I'm pretty sure Levi will want this white powder sent out for testing. I didn't want to disturb you while you were working, so I can come back later this afternoon and pick it up, if you agree to this. I can come back for any other reason too!

Followed by a happy face.

Wearing a foolish grin, she stared at that last line, trying to figure out what he meant. She tucked it against the side of her large writing pad and picked up her files, but it was hard to focus on work. She wondered about the sense of giving the drugs to Levi. At least they would be off her hands. Somebody needed to get the contents tested. That was the only way for sure to know what was going on.

She hadn't tracked down anybody missing the case. Now she didn't want to raise any alarms by asking too many questions. Things were touchy enough. Her gaze kept straying to Rory's note. Finally she had to tuck it out of sight before she could get down to work. Just before she was due to resume her appointments in the clinic again, her phone rang. "Hi, Levi. What's up?"

"I'm sending Rory back for the case," he said without hesitation. "I don't like the look of the images from the photos."

She dropped her pen and leaned back in her big office chair. "You're saying it's not safe here?"

"It's not safe to have that package. It's also likely not safe to *not* have the package," he said quietly. "It's hard to say which is worse. But, if these are drugs, we don't want them in circulation."

"I have animals and staff here. I can't have anybody endangered because of this."

"I'll call the local authorities and ask them to make more frequent drive-bys of your area. In the meantime, any chance you can call the delivery driver and tell him that he missed one?"

"No," she snapped. "Even the company said they weren't missing anything."

"What kind of an answer did you get?"

"It wasn't so much an answer as there was no data. They were missing nothing and had no record of this case of product."

"Interesting. Rory will be there soon. Sometime in the next couple hours."

"Thanks." She hung up and headed back to the clinic. She had a lot of work regardless of whatever else was going on. But that didn't stop her from keeping an eye out, seeing if Rory had shown up every time she made it back into the waiting room. When the afternoon passed by, and she saw no sign of him, she figured she had missed him.

Finally she poured herself a cup of coffee and returned to her desk. The last patient was gone, and her whole life was very narrowed and focused on the business. She had lots of help, but it wasn't enough sometimes. She had to do most of the paperwork herself. She went through files quickly, adding notes and making sure they were ready to be filed away again. After she was done, she checked her email. She took a look and shook her head as way too many appeared to be a priority.

She logged off and hung up her lab coat in the closet. She wondered if she should invest in converting the upstairs into an apartment to live here. But the longer she avoided doing it, the more she realized she needed to sometimes step away from the business; otherwise it took up too much of her life—it became her life and soul. She needed to have some outside outlet.

All the office staff had gone home already. The place was mostly dark.

She shook her head. "I didn't even see them leave," she murmured.

She checked on all the animals in back. She had none recovering from recent surgeries, so nobody needed to come in during the night. Normally she had somebody check at midnight and again at four in the morning.

She checked that the rear door was locked and that security was on before she stepped outside into the parking lot. The air was still heavy—muggy and humid. It was a shock after the air-conditioned interior of the clinic. She walked to her vehicle and stopped. A second vehicle was parked beside hers, one she recognized. Rory leaned against her small truck. He tipped his hat at her and nodded at her vehicle. "I can't believe you're the last one leaving."

She raised an eyebrow. "Why not? The business owners usually end up working way longer than the staff."

"Sure enough. It's the same for Levi and Ice. But I was hoping somebody would be with you."

"Do you think it's that dangerous here?" She looked around, realizing just how deserted the area was. She was surrounded by fields. Even if she screamed for help, no other building was nearby. No other people were about. It was a daunting thought. Yet, in a way, it was perfect for the animals. She had plenty of room for the dogs to be exercised, but she also had a section she kept for the large farm animals she worked on. The pasture opened to large stalls connecting to the rear of the clinic.

It was a unique combination and was one of the reasons she had bought the clinic. She'd always planned to bring a large animal veterinarian on board. Right now she was the only one doing both, but she couldn't handle all the work available.

She'd like to grow her business, and her services were needed locally, but, to do more, she needed to hire another vet. Currently she did the surgeries and call-outs while Jimmy, the other vet in her practice, took care of most of the patients in the clinic. Often it was more than they both could handle.

She could easily double the number of surgeries she performed. She had the room to expand as part of the clinic was closed off just because she didn't need the space at the moment. No point in having to clean two surgical rooms if she only needed the one. More clinical patient rooms were available as well. Her clinic was a huge building, and one she didn't utilize fully. She'd bought it with an eye to expanding down the road, but that depended on her ability to hire new staff. So far, she hadn't had much luck.

Like it would be nice to have someone else handle this current mess. She rubbed her temple. "You're making me nervous."

"Good," he said. "Can you open up again, so I can get that case?"

She sighed. "You could have come in five minutes ago, and then I wouldn't have had to set up the security."

He chuckled. "But this way I get to see if it works."

"What do you mean?"

"I want you to open the door but not shut off the alarm. You have a certain amount of time before the alarm goes off. How long before somebody responds to the alarm?"

She racked her brain for the answer. "I'm not sure. I think a phone call comes through within a couple minutes. If that isn't responded to, then a vehicle comes out."

"Well, let's see if the alarm goes off first," Rory said.

"But why wouldn't it?" she argued. She stepped in and pointed to the flashing lights on the alarm's keypad. "I have one minute to key in the code before the alarm goes off." She automatically went to do that, but he grabbed her hand and said, "Let's wait."

"Fine." She clapped her hands over her ears and waited. And waited.

Finally she dropped her hands, asking, "How did you know?"

But he wasn't at her side anymore. He went from window to window. Then she understood; he was checking to see which windows were wired as part of the security system. And her stomach sank. When she'd set up the system, she hadn't had tons of money and had done what she could but realized it wasn't enough. At least not now.

"Punch in the code to shut it off."

Instinctively she reached out to do it. Then, realizing how stupid her automatic reaction was, she asked, "Why did I shut it off if it's not working?"

"Just in case somebody puts the security system back online, we don't want it going off." He motioned her outside and said, "Lock up the door."

She quickly did, and he said, "Get in your vehicle, and go straight home. I'll follow you there."

She hopped inside and rolled down the window. "You are really scaring me."

"Good. Go now." He pounded on the hood of her vehicle and hopped into his truck. He was behind her before she even made it onto the main road. Her mind tried to figure out what exactly was going on as she made her way to the apartment she rented. She took her usual spot in the parking lot. Rory pulled into the guest space. He hopped out and said, "Let's go. Get inside your apartment so I can check it out before I leave."

"Check it out? Leave?"

He gave her a look and said, "I would love to stay, thanks. But I need to return to the clinic."

A sideways grin slid out, making her heart jump. Damn he was cute. She gave herself a headshake and asked, "But we just left it. I don't understand."

"Somebody has played with your clinic's security system. Considering that, no way you're hanging around that place alone. Because, if they got into the security system, they're watching the clinic too."

Bewildered at the quick change in her life, she led the way to the elevators and then up to the eighth floor. She got off with Rory at her side and walked to her corner apartment. She unlocked the door, opened it and stepped in. She waved a hand and said, "See? Everything is fine."

He ignored her and did a complete sweep of the apartment. The fact he was so thorough sent chills down her spine. He wasn't joking. He really thought she was in serious danger. She closed and locked the door behind her, just in case somebody came up behind them. She even hated to think that way. What the hell had happened to her life?

Finally he came back. "Stay here. I'll be back in a bit."

She raised both hands, her palms up. "Why are you coming back?"

"I have to deliver the pizza I ordered for our dinner of course. Lock up behind me, and don't let anyone in." He left without another word.

She almost wanted to phone Ice and ask what the hell Rory's problem was. However, she figured it would be harder to explain what she considered her reason for calling. She was tired, frustrated and, now, incredibly uneasy. She dropped her purse and keys where she always did and headed to her bedroom for a quick shower. When she came out, she was dressed in jeans and a T-shirt. She wasn't sure what the rest of night would bring, but, so far, the day had been absolutely crazy.

RORY DROVE PAST the vet clinic. He tried to look disinterested as he went by. He saw no sign of anybody, and, as far as he could tell, nobody hid in the hills. Yet every hair on the back of his neck stood up. He'd planned to return and do a drive-by regardless—to see if their leaving the clinic had brought anyone out of the woodwork. Not to mention he didn't like to leave the drugs behind. He really wanted to catch someone with them at the clinic.

"Ice, no sign of anyone here, but my instincts say they're here, watching."

"Flynn is in Houston and will take a look when he gets back. I might keep him for surveillance later. A fresh face no one will know."

"Somebody needs to go in without vehicles and keep watch on this place overnight."

"Since her security has been compromised, I'll get somebody there on the ground fast."

"There's a place up above where I can park and walk back. It's about a mile, maybe three-quarters of a mile."

"Good idea. Did you get the case?"

"I left it in the clinic. I figured if we caught them with it, that might be better."

"We don't want to lose it," she said, her tone sharp. "Do you know where it is?"

"I do."

"Good. Stay close to it until I can get someone else there. I don't want the other guys to get it."

He hung up, swerved into a small pullout off the road and parked his vehicle. He hopped out, jumped over the fence and ran for the tree line on the far side. He then inched his way along the ground. He looked at his clothes and realized he was hardly dressed to be unnoticeable. He yanked off his crisp white T-shirt, folded it into a small ball in his hand. His skin tone would blend in with the browns and golds of his surroundings better than the white T-shirt. Keeping low to the ground, he worked his way to the clinic.

He could see only two sides of the building, but the highway was in view, so he could also see it if anyone approached in a vehicle. He sat there for a good hour, figuring out any other angles to this mess. If somebody was selling drugs, how were they getting the packaging and the bottles? Was the company complicit, or was it completely unaware somebody was using its packaging to smuggle recreational drugs across state lines? Or across the border even. They needed to find out where the drugs were manufactured and packaged.

As he considered the angles, he jotted down notes on his phone. This stunk. The fact that anybody would even put animals in danger made him really angry. Of course the drugs were never intended for veterinarian use, but that didn't stop something from going wrong. If any of the animals were given any of those drugs, it would likely kill them within a few seconds. Thankfully they'd taken photos of the case showing the company label. Had Ice tracked anything down on the company? On the product? It had to be good enough to fool most people, but it hadn't been enough to fool Louise. Ice was already running the photo of the driver through the databases. Somebody had probably stolen the license plate for the delivery truck.

With perfect timing, Ice texted him. **Nothing off on company so far. The license plate came off a panel van stolen over six months ago.**

He whistled silently. That wasn't good. Now what they needed was this asshole to show up and go for the missing case of goods.

Rory waited. Just when he thought maybe his instincts had fooled him, he saw an old beat-up pickup truck roll down the road and go past the vet clinic. He could hear the engine slow as it pulled to the side of the road. Hopefully not in the same place he had parked. As he watched, two men walked back up the road and down the driveway to the clinic. They sauntered slowly as if they had every right to be here. Of course that was always the best way to approach the job. The minute you thought you looked suspicious, you were.

He crept closer as the men went into the front of the clinic. Damn, they'd gotten in fast. Did they have keys? Or just picked the lock? Worried they'd find the case, he reached the rear of the building and peered through one of the back windows. They were in the storeroom, speaking Spanish. His handle of the language wasn't bad, but their tones were muffled through the wall. He sent Ice a quick text. **Action.**

The men lifted and moved cases. So far they were on the wrong side of the room. Just then one of them turned and caught sight of him.

He dropped down, but it was too late. Shouts erupted from inside as footsteps raced toward the front entrance. This meant they hadn't cased the building as well as they should have because there was a back door closer to the storeroom. Of course maybe Rory was the one assuming too much. Maybe they knew something he didn't.

When nobody burst out of the back door, he quickly slid up against the door and peered in through the glass. No one was inside. He heard footsteps racing toward him along the path outside the building. He crept to the opposite corner and peered around. Saw the back of a man in jeans and a T-shirt, his hands on his hips. Rory crept up behind him and, with one blow, knocked him out.

He searched the man's pocket, checking for ID. The man didn't have a wallet, and, outside of keys and a few crumpled bills, his pockets were empty. Without anything on hand, Rory used his T-shirt to tie him up. With that done he took a precious moment and sent a text to Ice. He crept back toward the rear door. As he was about to open the door, he felt the hard metal of a gun pressed into the center of his back. "Don't move."

He slumped in place. *Damn it.* He hadn't been taken like that in a long time. And that pissed him right off. Sure, he'd taken out one, but this wouldn't make his day end on the right note. "What the hell do you want?"

"It's none of your business. What are you after?" the man replied.

"Something I know is hidden here," Rory said in a conspiratorial voice. "I came back to collect it."

The gun nudged him harder. "Collect what?"

"It's a vet clinic, dude." Rory snorted. "Drugs, man, drugs."

The man behind him prodded Rory again. "So you came to steal drugs from the animals?"

Rory had been in the business way too long to be fooled by that. "All drugs are good drugs, if you can sell them."

"Well, this is your lucky day in that I caught you and not one of the others in my crew. I'll give you one chance to get the hell out of here."

"Not without something for my troubles," Rory said. But now the gun was at the back of his neck.

"Oh, I think you'll change your mind. It's either get lost or take a bullet. So get lost and stay lost."

Rory raised his hands and let the guy push him to the front of the building. Just as they reached the corner, Rory turned and lashed out with his foot, nailing the gunman in the groin. As the man bent over, groaning, Rory grabbed his arm, twisting it up behind him and slamming him to the ground. With a knee to the center of his back, Rory held the gun to his head and said, "Shut the hell up."

The gunman swore fluently in Spanish until Rory shoved the gun harder against his ear. Finally the gunman went still.

"Now stay here," Rory snapped. "But thanks for the one chance to stay alive. You're lucky. I'll give you the same respect."

The gunman roared, "Who the fuck are you?"

"The guy who's getting the drugs I came for," Rory said calmly. He searched the man's pockets and found nothing—no wallet, no ID, no credit cards. Then Rory stripped the man's belt off. He quickly tied up his hands behind his back. Rory still needed to find a way to truss up the guy's feet. He pulled off the man's shoes, loosened the laces and used them to tie up the guy's ankles. If nothing else, it would slow him down. Then Rory stood, sent a text to Ice, walked inside to the back room and collected the drugs.

Hearing sirens in the far distance, he bolted out the back door. As soon as he reached the cover of the tree line, he called Ice and said, "I'm back in the trees. I have the case, and I left two turkeys trussed outside."

She laughed. "Okay, the sheriff's deputies are on their way. I've also contacted our favorite detective out of Houston, Detective Mannford."

"Good. Hope he gets here fast." Just then Rory heard a shot fired. He spun on his heels and said, "Shit."

"Was that gunfire?" Ice yelled.

"Yeah, it was."

A second hard pop filled the air.

"Oh, shit, Ice. I'm afraid the deputies will find dead men."

"That would not be good. Can you see the shooter?" she demanded. "Make sure you don't become the next victim."

"I can't see the shooter." Out of the corner of his eye, he saw movement. He spun to see a small figure race away. "Got him. Shooter heading north."

"I've got the deputies heading in that direction too. Return to the clinic and protect it. We don't want anybody else messing up the crime scene."

He was closer to his truck, so he dropped the case in the lockbox in the back and drove his truck to the front of the clinic. "I'm here now. Parked out front with the case." He walked outside while talking to her and swore. "One bullet to the back of the head of the first man." He ran around to the back and said, "I was right. A single bullet to the back of the head. Both men are dead."

"Okay, they were on an errand, likely under watch. When they failed, they outlived their usefulness," Ice said. "I don't like this at all."

Rory walked back to his truck. "How long until the authorities get here?"

"I'm not sure. Mannford said they were in the area on a call-out already."

Just then sirens whipped past. "A cruiser just passed, but it didn't come in to the clinic."

"Sit tight. I'm putting a call into Louise to make sure she stays inside her place and locked down."

"You do that. I'm holding tight here." He'd been right about the men making an attempt to recover the drugs. Unfortunately he hadn't expected the deadly punishment for failure. That took this to a whole new level.

And he'd left Louise alone—with pizza a forgotten meal. With this escalation, he didn't want to leave her for long, but he had to remain here until Mannford showed. Rory pocketed his phone and did a quick walk through the clinic. As far as he could see, nobody else had come in. That guy must have killed his men and left. Had he spoken to them first? Looked for the drugs? Or had he stepped up and shot them with the same clinical disinterest Rory had seen in so many other killers?

Two dead men was a game changer. Anyone who screwed up was taken out—clean and simple. But who the hell was behind this mess?

Chapter 3

LOUISE STOOD AT the glass doors to the small veranda off her living room. She stared in the direction of the clinic. She was just far enough away that she couldn't see the building. With her arms crossed over her chest, she thought about Ice's phone call. It was hard to believe now two dead men were at the clinic. Both of them killed by yet someone else. When she'd heard the news, she'd been afraid Rory had been attacked and was forced to kill someone. But, no, it couldn't be that simple. She reached up and scrubbed her face. "What the hell is going on?"

What bad luck that somebody had accidently unloaded a case of drugs at her place. Now she was caught in the middle, but, worse than that, so was everybody she worked with, and her patients. How had Rory known about the security system being compromised? He must have suspected tampering to test it as he had. And he'd been right. So that meant somebody had come in during the day and hacked the system. Or maybe it was possible to do that level of damage from outside.

She thought about how busy it had been today and how many people had come and gone. They had many friends and family walking outside as they waited for animal's to be cared for. Who knew what anyone was up to?

Levi's people were looking for a gunman planning things

out so he could come back to get what he wanted—when the clinic was empty. That was a saving grace for her patients and staff. The gunmen could have come in with guns blazing and hurt a lot of people *and* animals. It also made her realize how vulnerable the rest of her drug supply was. But then veterinarian clinics were notorious for getting broken into for the narcotics kept on hand. On the black market, they were worth a lot of money.

What was she supposed to do now? Ice had told her to sit still for the moment. Rory was waiting for the sheriff, and then he'd give a statement. That would take a bit of time; plus the bodies needed to be collected. As the owner she figured she'd be called to the clinic to speak with the deputies; however, Ice had told them Rory was "acting on her behalf."

That wasn't far off from the truth. She had brought Legendary Security into this mess. She wondered if Rory was in danger still. She pulled out her phone and sent Ice a message. **Does Rory need backup?**

The text came back almost immediately. **He's got it.**

Relieved, yet knowing she couldn't relax, she walked into the kitchen and put on coffee. It was late, but she hadn't eaten, and now her stomach churned with the endless possibilities of her immediate future. She should have just turned the drugs over to the sheriff in the first place. But then how would the bad guys have known she didn't have them in her possession anymore? It wasn't like she could put up a big sign on the highway, telling them to go see the local sheriff's office to collect their drugs. This had to be a decent-size operation if they had delivery trucks moving cases of the stuff. The question was, how the hell had it come to her place to begin with?

Why there? Unless it was a wrong address? A new driver who didn't know the route? There were too many possibilities, and her mind spun, endlessly looking for answers that weren't there. Half an hour later, while working on her second cup of coffee, Ice phoned her.

"The delivery truck has been found. It's on the outskirts of our side of Houston. The driver was shot dead. The vehicle was driven off the road and around a corner, where it was driven into a gully. So it took a little time to find."

"Oh, my God. Why was he killed? Because he failed?"

"That's usually the answer." Ice's voice was quiet, sad. As if she'd seen too many similar deaths over the years.

"What about the rest of the drugs?" Louise asked. "I presume there was no sign of them?"

"No. The back of the vehicle was empty."

"Of course it was. So he was supposed to deliver those drugs somewhere close by?"

"Possibly. And he gave you the wrong case."

"Well, I hope somebody figures it out fast," Louise said. "I don't want anybody else coming back and endangering the lives of the people who work for me or the animals. I run a busy clinic."

"I understand. The gunman wasn't there long. Just long enough to take out his cohorts. Rory doesn't think he took the time to look for the drugs. I don't know for sure. They may have decided the loss of the shipment wasn't worth getting caught over, or maybe, because they saw somebody was there, looking out for your interests, they wanted to disappear fast after the kills. So the guy's cleaning up. ... Three men are dead now."

"I wonder if he's done."

"Not likely. Not if this truly involves the drug trade.

Obviously we'll keep an eye on you. What we really need is to confirm the contents of those bottles. And we'll track them backward to find out where they were manufactured and packaged."

"Yes, I don't want those drugs to hit the streets."

"I think they've been returned to the drugs' distribution system, to empty out the contents, perhaps repackage them into a more saleable state. I highly doubt they were ever intended for animal use. That was just camouflage."

"That would be the one good thing in all of this. I'll be having nightmares about those drugs being given to my animals for a long time," Louise said. "Any update on Rory?"

"I think he's almost done with the deputies. He doesn't need to stay there. Once he secures the clinic, he'll return to your place. I'll have the clinic under surveillance all night."

"He doesn't need to come here. He's got to be tired by now," Louise offered.

"He'll stay with you until at least tomorrow. We need to figure out if anyone followed you home."

"That's why Rory was so careful when we arrived at the apartment. He was afraid somebody was coming after me. Wanting their drugs." She groaned out loud. "This is just an incredible state of affairs."

"It is. But this is what we do. In your case, you were just at the wrong place at the wrong time."

"Yeah, well, I'd like very much to get back to being at the right place at the right time."

"You are. Sit tight. Make sure you confirm it's Rory before you open the door." With that, Ice hung up.

Louise sat on the couch for another hour. Then there was a knock on the door. Almost immediately, she received a text. She pulled out her phone and checked it. *Rory.* The text read **I'm at the door**.

She smiled, looked through the peephole, and, indeed, it was him. She unlocked and then unbolted the door. "You know, for a pizza delivery man," she said, trying for a note of humor, "you're pretty late."

He nodded. "Isn't that the truth?" Entering, he said, "Shut and lock the door behind me please." He walked the two large boxes of pizza to the kitchen table and said, "Did you eat?" He turned to study her face as he slipped the hat off his head and placed it on the far side of the table.

"No, I couldn't. Ice has kept me up to date with the news."

"Good, then I don't have to tell you."

She brought over the coffeepot and poured him a cup. "Here's some coffee, although it's past its prime." She sat down at the kitchen table. "You didn't see the killer?"

"No. I didn't. I had no idea there was a third man at all," he said. "Believe me. I feel pretty shitty about that too."

"Too?"

He gave her a hard glance. "Two men died tonight because I knocked them out and tied them up. If they hadn't failed in their jobs, they would be alive right now."

That was a side of him and this situation she hadn't considered. "Well, I'm glad the killing weighs on you. It should never be an easy thing. At the same time, they broke into my clinic to get illegal drugs. I don't think they would have given you the same kind of consideration."

He studied her for a long moment, then nodded. "One did, actually." He gave her a quick explanation, then added, "But I doubt that largesse would have lasted." He nodded at the pizza as he flipped open the box. "I'm starved. I didn't know what you might like. So I brought two choices."

She looked at the pizza in front of her with more toppings on it than she'd ever imagined could fit. "What is that? Everything but the kitchen sink?" she joked.

"Almost." He reached into the box, and, holding the piece with two hands, he took a big bite.

The second offering had less varied toppings and lots of pepperoni. She chose one of those. "I can't remember the last time I had pizza," she said and took a bite. Almost immediately her taste buds exploded with flavor. Melted cheese, warm sauce and hot spicy pepperoni filled her mouth.

"How is it?" Rory mumbled around his piece.

She grinned. "This one is good. I don't know about that other one. How can you taste anything when there's so much on it?"

"It's a package deal," he said. He finished his first piece, reached across to the second box and grabbed the largest of the pepperoni slices. As she slowly finished her smaller piece, she stared at him. "How is it you can eat so much?"

He glanced at her, affronted. "You don't even know how much I eat. Besides, look at that little bite you've had. You need way more than that to keep going."

The truth was, she didn't. She'd never been a big eater, but she'd always enjoyed watching others enjoy their food. She figured, as long as she was full, that was all that counted. For the next few minutes, they ate in silence. She tried the smallest piece from the heavily laden pizza and admitted, "That's actually really good."

"See?"

As he reached for his fourth piece, she finished her coffee and refilled her cup. "Now what?"

He shrugged. "The sheriff has the drugs and the two dead men and knows about the third dead guy. I rigged together your security system for tonight. You'll have to call the company tomorrow to install a good lockbox system for the drugs. If thieves get past the security system, you'll want a second deterrent to accessing the drugs in the cupboard."

She nodded. "I've spent a lot of time thinking about my security system. Any intruder is likely after the drugs and not the animals, but I'd feel terrible if anyone hurt the animals while trying to get at the drugs."

"Upgrading the security will be expensive though," he warned.

"Isn't it always?" She sat back and watched as he proceeded to pick up his seventh piece. "Were you expecting company?" she asked, motioning at the still half-packed boxes of pizza.

He shook his head. "I hope not. There isn't enough to share." When he was finally full, he settled back and grinned. "That's just about the right amount for tomorrow's breakfast."

She chuckled and then stopped. "Are you staying the night?" Ice had said that, but the notion hadn't really clicked. What would it be like to have him stay here with her?

"Sure I am."

"You don't have to, you know. I'll be fine."

He shook his head. "Nope. I'm staying."

"Why?"

"Maybe it's not for you," he said craftily. "Maybe it's for Rose, the puppy."

"The puppy?" She stared at him in confusion, not understanding the swift shift in conversation.

He chuckled. "She's pretty special. I've got to make sure you're still around to look after her."

"What she is, is a heartbreaker. Don't forget Anna is looking for families for those dogs." She hated to remind him but knew the puppies would find permanent homes and most likely were not staying at the compound. No way would Levi let all six puppies remain there. Of course, she'd seen miracles before.

"I know. That'll hurt. The women are going nuts over them. Then so is Alfred. Anna must have caught Levi in a weak moment to get him to agree to keep the puppies even for a while."

She shook her head. "Yet here you're doing all this for Rose."

He shrugged. "We can't have Rose suffering because you aren't there to look after her." He flashed a big wicked grin and said, "Do you mind if I have more coffee?"

She felt like a horrible hostess. He had brought dinner. She stood. "Why don't we take it into the living room?"

With full cups, they sat down on the couch, and she rested her feet on the coffee table. "Is there anything to be done overnight?"

"Ice and Levi are on it. We've got two men watching the place. The gunman left before the sheriff's deputies arrived and may not know the authorities now have the drugs, and that will bring someone back to double-check. I'm sure."

"As much as that terrifies me, I hope they do," she admitted. "Maybe you guys can capture them this time. Getting answers and making this all go away works for me."

"It's hard to say," he admitted. "If they capture somebody, he might realize the price the others have already paid and not talk at all."

"But, if he is in custody, he should be safe."

He gave her a flat look and asked, "Do you really believe

that?"

With a wince, she sagged back and shook her head. "I guess, if somebody is determined enough, they'll get him wherever he is."

"Exactly." He glanced at his watch. "It's after ten now. Actually it's almost eleven." He frowned and stared off in the distance, as if thinking.

"Bedtime?" she asked, standing and walking to the kitchen.

"What time do you get up in the morning?"

"I have to be at the clinic before eight-thirty."

"Okay, if you're ready, let's head to bed. We both need sleep. The guys are taking shifts watching over the clinic. I don't know for sure, but I might get a call-out. I need to grab a few hours while I can."

Silently she dumped the rest of her cold coffee down the sink and pulled out blankets and pillows from the hall closet. "Will this be okay for the night? The couch isn't very big," she said, staring at the sofa that seemed to take up a ton of space in the small living room when she had first bought it and now looked like a love seat relative to Rory.

"It'll be fine."

She nodded. In her room she stood for a long moment and then tucked herself into bed. She didn't know what kind of night it would be for him or for her. Hopefully she'd sleep.

RORY CRASHED ON the couch and didn't wake up for several hours. When his phone buzzed beside his head, he instinctively reached for it and pulled up the message. It was two o'clock in the morning. He read the All Clear message, dropped the phone back onto the table and closed his eyes again.

When he woke up again, it was almost six. He checked his phone, but, outside of another All Clear message, there was nothing. He stretched and sat up. After going to the bathroom, he stood in front of the coffeemaker and figured out how much coffee grounds to use. The pot was smaller than he was used to. He judged the coffee as best he could, turned it on and then stepped onto the small veranda to clear his head.

Louise appeared to be still asleep. He checked his watch. He could give her a bit longer. She had another long day ahead of her. Just being at the clinic would be difficult. She'd be worried about more intruders—or worse, another gunman. Somebody had messed up her security system and most likely during the day while the clinic was open. It was a busy place. It would be easy to overlook a single man. Rory wanted to go back with her and run through the security feed.

He sent a message to Ice, giving her a status update and his plans to head to the clinic with Louise soon.

Check the camera feed while you're there was her response.

He smiled and said, "That's the thing about working with pros. You're always on the same wavelength, all the time. It also means you never have an original idea because everybody else is thinking the same thing."

Still, it was all good. He turned when he heard the bedroom door open. As he watched, Louise stepped out fully dressed and ready to go to work. She gave him a wan smile and said, "I hope you slept well. Honestly, from my perspective, it was a shitty night."

He nodded. "Let's hope it's the only bad one we have."

She looked at him and asked, "What are we doing this morning?"

"Having coffee and pizza and then heading to work. I'm coming with you. I want to go over your security feed and see if I can figure out who disabled it."

She smiled. "Not a bad way to start the day."

Chapter 4

LOUISE WALKED OUTSIDE to her car. She took a moment to inhale the fresh air. Talk about a disruptive night. That was without considering her male houseguest. Larger than life, Rory wasn't someone to ignore. Just then Rory stopped beside her and looked at her carefully. She smiled at him. "I'm fine."

He nodded. "I know. Just wondering if something new was going on."

She gave a half laugh. "No, there doesn't need to be anything new to still be something. My life is often chaotic." She motioned to her truck. "Is there any point in going to the clinic outside of checking on the animals and any damage to the clinic? Am I allowed to open today?"

"Absolutely. Hopefully the deputies are done. If you've got appointments and animals coming in, then you'll need to look after them or move all the appointments to another day."

"Right. That's not fun, so let's hope I don't have to resort to that." Louise got into her vehicle, turned on the engine, aware Rory stood right beside her, waiting. He would follow her into work, and maybe that was a good thing. She'd certainly been to hell and back emotionally after finding out two men had been killed at her clinic. She'd slept ... but badly. She briefly considered closing up shop, but she offered a valuable service and couldn't stand to think of leaving all those animals in need.

It only took ten minutes to get to the clinic. She drove slowly as she approached the parking lot. Nancy, her front desk assistant, was already there, looking worried. The relief that crossed her face when Louise pulled up was almost comical. Then she recognized another man from Levi's compound who stood behind Nancy. Louise hopped out and walked over to him with a big smile. "Hi, Logan."

"Hi, Louise," Logan said with a big grin. "Only you and Anna can get into so much trouble."

She groaned. "We're not doing it on purpose."

"Didn't say that," Logan said with a shake of his head. "Sometimes you ladies are just trouble magnets."

At the sound of a truck she turned to watch Rory pull in and park. He stepped out, and the two men exchanged greetings.

Pushing back the brim of his hat, Rory asked, "Anything new?"

Logan shook his head. "The deputies left several hours ago."

"Any reason she can't stay and open up today?"

"I asked them specifically, and they said she can continue with business but to keep an eye out. And to get her security system fixed as fast as possible."

Louise frowned, surprised they were okay with her opening up. "Is that normal when two men were murdered?"

Her assistant gasped in horror. "What? Somebody was killed?"

Rory gently squeezed Louise's shoulder. "They were shot outside," he said to her assistant. "There was a break-in and a falling out among thieves, leaving two dead and the killer on the run."

Nancy shook her head and wrapped her arms tightly around her very ample frame. "Well, we need to get in there and make sure nobody is hurt."

"If you mean the animals," Logan said, "they're doing just fine."

He stepped out of the way, and Nancy bustled inside. Louise followed her but much more slowly. She stopped at the security system by the back door and said, "Did they damage the system here or outside?"

"Both," Logan said quietly. "The deputies collected fingerprints. They'll have to fingerprint everybody who works for you, just to rule them out."

She nodded. "But that also would then imply somebody else had made it this far back in my clinic, right?"

Both men nodded. Logan spoke first. "I was just starting to explore that when Nancy arrived. She was pretty upset to see me here. Of course, if I'd left the crime scene tape up from the sheriff's deputies, she would have been more upset," he said with a lopsided grin at Louise.

"Very true. Thank you for that." She watched as Rory looked around, as if comparing what he'd seen last night to what he was looking at right now.

In a low voice he asked Logan, "Did you find anything?"

Logan shook his head. "I arrived just after you left. I stayed out back, keeping an eye on the place from a distance. Then I moved in when the deputies looked like they were leaving. I explained to the officers who I was and why I was here."

Louise thought about that comment and realized they probably worked with the local authorities a lot. Maybe she had gone to the right people for help after all. But it also reminded her how normal this was for these men. "So, is it supposed to be just another day?" she asked. "That seems almost disrespectful. Two men died here last night."

"They did but not by your hand and not by our hand—by the lifestyle they led. Obviously we don't want to take it lightly, but I highly doubt you want to make it obvious to anybody what they were doing here. If you can't keep your place secure, how will you keep anyone's beloved pet safe?"

She shuddered. "I see what you mean." Trying to shake that off, she walked into the back room and checked on the animals. Nancy already had the big bunny in her arms, giving it a cuddle. She looked up when Louise walked in. "They all appear to be just fine."

Louise nodded. "I didn't expect anything different. The men were checking here off and on throughout the night."

"It's such a terrible thing," Nancy said. "Why now?"

Louise wasn't sure if she should mention the drugs. As she looked up, she caught Rory's gaze and his very slight head shake. She realized he wanted her to keep quiet. It was probably the smartest thing, but she hated lying to her staff. Most of them had been with her since she had bought the place. They were good people and deserved the truth. In a calm voice she said, "In a way we're lucky it hasn't happened before, especially with us so secluded here. Lots of veterinarian clinics get broken into for their drugs."

"But never ours," Nancy said stoutly. "Either we've been lucky or our security has been too good."

"Regardless, Rory and Logan will inspect our security and see what we need to upgrade," Louise said with a smile. "Don't worry. We'll fix this. Nothing concerns me more than our safety and the safety of our patients."

Louise turned her attention to a big tomcat that had gotten an infection after he went home from surgery. "He's looking much better," she said in an attempt to change the conversation.

Nancy smiled. "He's a big healthy boy. He should be doing just fine." Together they pulled out the big tomcat, and his engine kicked in. "I guess he's happy to be going home today." Nancy chuckled. "I should give his owners a call and make sure they're coming."

"Given the situation, it's probably a good idea if we send home as many as we can."

"Do you think the men will come back?"

"I highly doubt it. But the fact that it's happened once is too many times," Louise said in a darker voice.

Nancy nodded. "I'm with you there." She turned and carried on with her day.

Louise headed to where the drugs were kept. She found both Logan and Rory at the back door, eyeing the security keypad there. "Any suggestions on how to fix this?" she asked.

"Honestly, if somebody wants in, they'll get in," Rory said. "This cabinet won't keep anybody out as the locks are easily broken, so it's more a case of adding another layer of protection in front. Once you have a decent security system that's fully operational, that will help as well."

"What do I need to do to improve the security?" She groaned, feeling a headache coming on. "I thought I had a good system."

"You did," Logan said, "until you got involved in this mess. Some things you'll never keep people out of. When they have that need to get inside, they will get inside. So you do the best you can and hope it's enough."

"That's not the answer I'm looking for," she snapped.

"Of course it's not," Rory said. "On the other hand, let's see if we can get a quote from the security company on moving your system up a level."

She winced at the thought of more expenses. "Business is decent, but I already have a ton of overhead costs."

"I know," Rory said gently. "But, like you said, you don't want this to happen again."

"Is it likely to?"

At that Rory laughed. "If we could tell you that, we'd make a killing in the fortune-telling business," he said. "Honestly, until this is over, you need to have the best security you can afford."

"So should I hire a security guard overnight? Would that even be the answer? If these guys seem to think the drugs are still here, won't they come back?"

"That's possible," Rory said. "And, if that's the case, then we need to talk to Levi."

She shook her head. "You guys do all kinds of big badass work. I can't begin to afford your services." She waved her hand at Logan standing there with a half smirk on his face. "I don't even know what I owe him for last night."

Rory nodded. "Only one way to find out." He pulled out his phone and hit Ice's number.

Louise wanted to growl in frustration. "This is a talk I'm really not prepared to have right now."

"Maybe not," he said cheerfully. "But it's bothering you. So let's solve it now so it doesn't stress you out more."

She rolled her eyes at him and glared at Logan who, by now, was grinning like a fool. "What is so funny?" she snapped.

Logan chuckled out loud. "There's nothing funny about the situation," he corrected, "but about you and him there definitely is."

She looked at Logan for a moment and then at Rory's puzzled frown and said, "See? Rory doesn't understand what the hell you're talking about either."

Logan chuckled again. "Not a biggie. You'll see eventually."

She glanced over at Rory again to see if he had any idea what Logan was talking about. But he was already answering his phone. He'd walked several feet away, as if he could hear better, but she figured it was a private conversation she wasn't supposed to hear. She appreciated everything he was doing, but she really hated being beholden to anybody. She understood the value of pro bono work. After all she looked after Anna's animals, and she did most of that pro bono. Whenever Anna could raise money to cover any of the vet fees, Louise used it to cover the expenses only, never her labor. As far as she was concerned, every vet should do their job to help out where they could. But that didn't apply in this case.

Rory suddenly turned to look at her, but he kept talking.

Logan reached out a hand and said, "Let him deal with it."

"Why?" she asked, raising her eyebrows as she studied his features.

"Because it would be good for Rory. He's fairly new to the team. This gives him something to focus on, to take the lead on."

She didn't understand how that worked. She'd known he was a recent addition to the compound, just not how long. "How new?"

"That day you met him at our place was his first day. He just came from helping out at his family's ranch. His brother was in a major accident, and Rory took over until his brother was back on his feet again."

Her heart warmed. "He's not all bad then, huh?" she said with a happy grin.

"No, Rory is one of the good guys." As he walked closer to Rory, he turned his head to her and said, "You could do much worse."

She stared at him in shock, which quickly turned to horror and then to outrage. "Oh, no, you don't," she snapped. "Don't even start down that path."

But he wasn't listening. His head was bent toward Rory, listening in on his call.

RORY LISTENED AS Ice and Levi talked in the background. Logan had joined him.

"Any decision?" Logan asked.

Rory held the phone between the two of them. "They're discussing the issue."

When Ice came back on the line, Logan leaned close and said, "Ice, Logan here. You do know she does all the work for Anna and Flynn's place for free, right?"

Ice's voice was dry as she said, "I did know that. *I*, on the other hand, still have bills to pay."

The two men winced. "You can take my wages off the ticket for this one," Rory said. "I watched those men. It doesn't thrill me in the least to see her left like this."

Beside him, Logan chuckled. Rory shot him a look and told Ice, "After last night, I won't leave her in the lurch just because she doesn't have the funds for this. Nobody has funds for round-the-clock security."

Logan nodded.

Ice said, "Let me talk to her, please."

Interesting. Rory handed the phone to Louise. "Ice wants to talk to you."

She took the phone from his hand and said, "Hi, Ice. What's up?"

Rory could hear the forced note of lightness in Louise's tone. She was seriously worried about this. Security was expensive. Rory had no idea what Levi would charge Louise for hours already billed. Then there was a security upgrade that could run into several thousand dollars; plus she had insurance deductibles to meet. After this incident, her premiums would go up. Although, with any luck, she should be fully covered for the destroyed security system and any other physical damage. The two men waited until the phone call concluded.

Whatever the end result was, Louise had a look of relief on her face, as she was smiling. "That's awesome. Thank you very much." She handed the phone back to Rory. "I don't know what you said, but the charge will be doable."

"And that's what matters," Rory said. "This won't last forever, but, while we're in the middle of fixing things, let's not cut corners and get anybody else hurt."

She nodded. "While I get back to my patients, maybe you guys could figure out what the hell is going on with the security system and what I might need to fix it."

The two men headed to the front door. The waiting room was filling up. Logan took a look. "She's got a busy practice here."

"Yeah, she does. According to what I saw, her rates are reasonable too."

Logan nodded. "Anna sings Louise's praises all the time. Louise cuts Anna a deal on just about everything she possibly can."

"Does your dad pick up the tab for the rest?" Rory asked. "Gunner's generosity is well-known in many corners."

Logan gave him a lopsided grin. "There has to be some advantages to having money. If we can't help those in need, then what is it for?"

Rory agreed. It was nice to know good men populated their personal lives and not just their work lives. He motioned to the electrical panel in the back. "This is a pretty basic system."

"They probably charged her a fortune for it." Logan tapped his foot. "You know? We have the equipment at home. We can probably set up a better system for cheaper." He turned to look at Rory. "I wonder if Ice and Levi have considered going into the security system business. They're set up for it. We could install a system, and it could be monitored from the compound."

The two men stared at each other, both liking the idea. "I wonder what the liability is on something like that."

"Well, if they haven't figured it out by now, you know it won't take Ice very long. They already have massive liability insurance."

"What about Anna and Flynn? Do they have a security system there?"

Logan looked at him in surprise, his eyebrows rising. "They do indeed, and you're right. It's connected to our system." He pulled out his phone, dialed and said, "Levi, Anna and Flynn are connected to our state-of-the-art system at home, right?"

Rory could just about hear Levi's affirmative answer.

"How about we set up this clinic to do the same? Have you guys considered doing something like that on a commercial level?"

"Not commercially," Levi said. "Don't have the time and the manpower."

"But you have it around Michael's new place, and you have it at Anna and Flynn's. You'd probably also do it for anybody else who needs to set up a property around the area. Right?"

"Possibly ..." Levi said on a groan. "You guys are killing me, you know that?"

The two men grinned. "In about an hour we can take out this Mickey Mouse system she's got here, which is seriously underperforming for her requirements. We have the right equipment at home. We can put it together, wire it for her and hook it up to the console in the control room at the compound."

"She hasn't had a break-in for all the time she's been here. It's only because of this current issue," Rory added. "Meaning, monitoring the clinic wouldn't take much man-hours on a daily basis."

"Let me talk to Ice, and we'll get back to you."

"That's actually a good idea," Rory said to Logan after Levi hung up. "We also have to consider the fact we can't just make a change like this without Louise's permission. Maybe she doesn't want to be involved with Levi to that extent."

"Yet they've got the best security system in the area," Logan said.

"Does she know that though?" Rory frowned. He turned toward the offices and the patient rooms. A steady stream of people came and went. "We won't be able to question her anytime soon. Let's just analyze what she needs, so she can get a price quote on what it would cost to replace and upgrade her system with her current company. We'll get Ice to do the same. Then Levi and Ice can sort out what they would need to do to make it happen."

"It would be a really good sideline for them."

"It's hardly a sideline. This is what we do all over the place."

Logan shook his head. "You have no idea how many people we've helped because of their shitty security systems."

"The problem is, nobody really thinks about it until it's too late. Then they've got a mess on their hands and need to get it fixed and fixed fast. At that point, they generally don't fuss about the money. They want a solution that'll work and keep them safe."

"Just like Louise."

It took an hour for them to check the lines to see which windows were covered, which doors were covered. By the end of it, Logan was pretty disgusted. "This is beyond rudimental. She needs a massive upgrade. With just a couple wires cut, the whole thing shuts down."

Rory was of the same opinion.

Just then Trish, one of the vet assistants, walked over. "Somebody is out front from the security company. Louise asked if you could take care of it. Get quotes for what she needs, and she'll talk to you during her lunch break."

Rory grinned. "Perfect. We just finished our analysis here."

The two walked out front to meet the security person called in to look at the system. They took him back to go over it.

The security rep said, "I can give you a quote before I leave. We're looking at several thousand dollars obviously, and she'd need to upgrade to being monitored. That will mean her monthly fee will move to a new plan."

"Okay. Give us a quote, and Louise can make a decision." They discussed video feeds and alarm systems routed back to the main headquarters. By the time they were done, they had a much better idea of what the security company could provide. As the security technician walked to his service van, Rory said, "Well, that won't do the job."

Logan laughed. "Sometimes I think our background makes us more paranoid than anybody. But you're right. This system sucks, and he's not the one to do this properly."

"Do you think we can get anybody else to give us a hand?"

"Flynn got in late last night. Ice is keeping him as backup. It's not like we need the help. But I know he'd be here in a heartbeat to help out Louise."

Rory brightened. "That's right. It would be a good opportunity for him to pay Louise back."

"Absolutely. No way would Flynn and Anna leave Louise in trouble like this. Not if they want to continue getting her assistance. Another break-in could shut her down, if not permanently, at least temporarily."

Rory winced. "True enough. Can you call him? Let's get all our information ready, so we can talk to her at lunch."

Logan nodded. "You call Ice, and I'll call Flynn."

Rory rolled his eyes at that. He definitely wasn't getting the easy part of the bargain. On the other hand, he believed in what he was fighting for, and that made all the difference. He pulled out his phone once again, flicked the password swipe to the side and clicked on the office number. When Ice answered, he said, "We need to talk."

Chapter 5

LOUISE KNEW SHE was lucky to already know Levi and Ice. That they were helping her through this was huge. She'd wondered about asking Flynn for a favor but didn't like how she felt as if she were now calling in her marker. Because that wasn't who she was. She truly believed in service to others. In her case particularly service to animals. She'd help any animal in need. People, well, not so much. But sometimes the two went hand in hand.

There was a knock on her open door. She looked up to see the two men standing in front of her. "Is it lunchtime already?"

"No, it's past lunch. You ran late."

She glanced at her watch and leaned back with a tired smile and said, "That happens a lot."

But the men looked like they were on a mission. Rory almost bounced with good news. She eyed them suspiciously. "What are you looking so happy about?" she demanded.

Both men grinned. "We just expanded Levi's business model for him."

She leaned forward. "What?"

Logan chuckled. "Well, they already handle the security for Anna and Flynn's place."

She turned her gaze from one to the other. "They do? I didn't think Levi and Ice were in the security system business."

"They're already in the security industry," Rory said.

Right. Of course they were. She nodded as if she understood.

Rory chuckled, obviously not taken in. "They handle security for people, families, companies and governments all over the world," he said by way of a short explanation. "But that can fall under many different umbrellas."

That still didn't make a ton of sense to her, but she knew whatever they did was big. In her mind, she likened them to a secret government operation. She knew they had no affiliations with the government, but she had heard rumors that Levi and Ice maintained lots of relationships there. And not just within their government but many others. "What does this have to do with me?" she asked.

"We suggested to Levi that he consider putting your place under his same security umbrella. And, after speaking with your security company tech, we can do a much more comprehensive job for less money."

She sat back and stared. "Is that possible?" Inside her joy and relief dominated because she knew her clinic, and all those in it, would be safe. As a solution to her current problems, that would be huge. Levi was a pro and could look after her place at a whole new level. He wasn't just offering the residential crap, which she began to understand most affordable security systems were. He really took the whole process seriously. Her new system would be on steroids. At that reminder, she winced inwardly. "Wouldn't that be very expensive?" she asked cautiously. "I don't have the money for this. And you guys do seem to like the best of the best when it comes to equipment."

"Levi knows that," Logan said. "Of course they can't do

this for free."

She snorted. "You think? Neither can I."

"You do a lot of free things for Anna and Flynn."

She frowned, not liking it brought up. "How do you know that?"

Logan rolled his eyes.

"Okay. So I help out sometimes with different animals." She shrugged in irritation. "It's hard to get funding for places like Anna's, and the animals need treatment. Plus we would be overrun with puppies and kittens if somebody didn't help," she exclaimed, trying to rein in her emotions. Her tone was irritable, defensive, even though she tried hard not to let it be. It was an old beef with her. People had enough money to buy fancy coffees every day of the month but argued about handing over five bucks toward fixing a cat or feeding a kitten.

"We understand that. It's a fact. Levi also does a lot of pro bono work."

"I'm pretty sure the price they're charging me already counts as pro bono work," she said in disgust. "I can't ask them to help anymore."

"Oh, you'd be paying," Rory said. "But Ice put together a proposal that's pretty much the same as what you're paying now. Only you'd be getting much better equipment, a much higher level of security and, of course, Levi and Ice as backup."

She frowned. "What are you talking about?"

Logan took up the story. By the time they explained everything they had planned for her physical upgrade and then compared the coverage offered by the old system to the new services she'd receive on a monthly basis, she was gob-smacked to discover the price they estimated was nearly the same as she paid currently. Of course that was without a confirmation from Ice. She turned on her computer, flicked through the files, bringing up her security folder containing the current contract and invoices.

"Are you sure this isn't a charity job?" she asked, frowning as she studied the figures in front of her. "I'm paying a bit less than that right now, but, as you obviously know, it's a pretty crappy system."

"It is. Levi will send you a new quote to upgrade your system to what you should have, according to him. Then you'll need the quote from your current company to make an informed decision."

An email from Levi popped into her inbox. "It's here now. Just a sec."

She took a look, read the few itemized issues, one of which was simply equipment, and the other was the ongoing monthly service fee. The total was only a little more than what she currently paid and was very close to the estimate Rory had given her. She glanced back at the rough estimate from her current company, and her eyebrows rose. "Well, I can tell you right now that I can't afford what my current company wants," she exclaimed. "How is it Ice and Levi can do it for less?"

"Because they know what they're doing for one. If you're up for it, we'll get started today."

She looked at Rory. "That fast?"

The two men gave her a droll look. "It's what we do."

She thought back to the original installation and hookups. It took them a week to just show up. It could be a really good thing having Levi and Ice handle her system. She smiled and said, "As long as that figure is good, I'm all for it."

"Then call her," Rory urged. "Do it now, and then we can get this done and in place."

"Completed this afternoon?"

Both men shook their heads. "No, but we could have it set up by the end of tomorrow. It depends on the equipment. We could be short a few connections. We will have to see what else we need that Levi doesn't already have on hand."

It was all over her head as she listened to them talk about it. She was already reaching for her cell phone. She called Ice and said, "Are you sure about this? It seems awfully cheap."

Ice's beautiful laughter rippled through the phone. "Glad to hear you think that. Does that mean it's a yes?"

"Are you sure you want to do this open-ended?"

"I was thinking of a trial. How about one year? Then we can sit down and reevaluate."

"Perfect," Louise said with a big smile. "That at least gets me out of this trouble. Let's go ahead and do it."

"Good. Tell the men to come home. No, wait." Ice stopped and was silent for a moment. "Send Logan home. He can collect the equipment. Rory should stay right now. I've asked the sheriff's office to circle by there several times during the day and the night too."

"Will do."

Beaming, she turned to the men and said, "Logan, you are to go home. Rory, you are to stay here. Deputies to do more drive-bys."

Both men nodded. "That's what we expected."

Logan turned away, saying, "I'll be back as soon as I collect what we need."

Rory looked at Louise. "You didn't bring lunch, and you didn't have any pizza for breakfast. What do you plan on doing about food?"

Instantly half of her good feelings fell away. "You're not my babysitter."

His eyebrows shot upward. "The hell I'm not. Right now, and particularly until we get this system set up, you're as vulnerable as anybody can be."

Her heart sank as she stared out the window. "I could go somewhere for lunch, but nothing close by appeals."

"There's a good family restaurant not that far away," he suggested. "Let's go."

"You don't have to go with me," she protested. It was kind of odd to have somebody like him around all the time. Reassuring but also ... odd.

He just shook his head but stood stalwart in front of her.

With a heavy sigh, she stood. "Let me check when my next patient is. We have to be back for that."

He walked with her to the reception area. They had an hour and fifteen minutes. "Good. That's enough time to get you some real food." Taking her arm, he ushered her out the front door and into his truck.

With a heavy sigh, she sat down in the front seat. "I hadn't realized how tired I am," she admitted.

"Fatigue is worse when you don't eat," he said gently. "You should know that from the animals. Just sit back and relax. Close your eyes. We will be there in a few minutes."

She let her eyes slide closed as her emotions settled into a more balanced and calm place as her earlier stresses about illegal drugs, killers, break-ins and her lack of money swept away. So much had gone on during the last twenty-four hours. She was amazed at the speed of all the events, and, at the same time, she was overwhelmed with Levi and Ice's generosity. She didn't know how she would repay them.

That worry pounded away in the back of her head. They were good people, but they shouldn't be picking up the tab for her.

Beside her Rory murmured, "The idea of closing your eyes is to rest, not to sit there and fuss."

She rolled her head sideways toward him and said, "How did you know I wasn't napping?"

He took a hand off the wheel and covered hers. And that was when she realized her fists were clenched together. She stared down at them, easing up her hold and said, "I'm not used to taking charity."

He laughed. "You're not used to asking for help when you need it either, are you?"

She frowned. "I haven't had to do much of that."

"Then you're lucky," he said. "Not everybody has that option. We all need help sometime. So accept it gracefully, and let's get this dealt with."

She smiled. "Are you always so pragmatic?"

"I'm a realist. Shit happens. We don't always have a shovel to clean it up. We do the best we can until we can get one."

At that she burst out laughing. "Well, this is definitely a shit storm."

"Hey, if we're lucky, the worst has already passed."

"Amen to that."

He pulled into the parking lot of the restaurant.

"I wonder if anything here won't kill my arteries?" she asked.

"There sure is, and, even if there wasn't, you need energy, and you need carbs. There is a time to worry about your arteries and a time not to worry about them," he said. "Remember, Doc. You've got to pick your fights."

She laughed. "You're good for me."

He chuckled. "I absolutely am. Now remember that as we start working together."

"What? You mean I'll see you even more than I do now?"

"Yep. I'll be in your face for the next day or so."

RORY OPENED THE truck door for her and helped her out. She looked at him in surprise. He shrugged. "My mother raised me to be a gentleman."

She chuckled. "Good for your mother. It's almost a lost art."

He held the door open for her as they went into the restaurant too. "I've never been here before," she said, looking around.

"I have. A couple times. They have a really good soup-and-salad deal. If you want nothing else, that's good hearty food for the stomach."

"As long as gallons of coffee go with it, I will be a happy diner."

Once seated, Rory dropped his hat on the chair beside them. The waitress arrived with menus. Louise studied the brightly colored pictures and had no trouble picking out a favorite. After they ordered, Louise turned her attention to her companion. "You've gone way beyond what was required to help me out," she said quietly. "I want you to know I appreciate your part in that."

"No problem." He grinned at her. "Happy to help."

She nodded. "Any news on the men who were killed?"

He shook his head. "We've been a little busy this morning. I can check if you want."

She nodded. "Please do."

He sent a text to Ice and Levi, letting them know Louise was looking for an update. Ice's response came back immediately. "Both men from your break-in have been identified," he read quietly. "Both have criminal records."

She sighed. "From drugs?"

"Ice doesn't say," he said. "It's probably too early to know those details, plus the ID on the third guy, your delivery driver."

She nodded. "I need to go to the sheriff's office and give a statement, don't I?"

"I think Ice said something about them stopping at the clinic later this afternoon. They want to talk to you." He glanced at the table and then patted her hand.

She looked down and realized she was clenching the coffee cup so tightly that her knuckles were white. She sighed and relaxed. "I don't have anything to add to the case."

"Yes, you do. You need to tell them about the delivery driver and the case of drugs."

She winced. "I wish I'd never seen him. If only he hadn't mixed up my order … It's just a big nightmare." She stared out the window.

He hated to see the frown lines on her face. She looked tired, but, then again, almost every time he saw her, she looked tired. She really wore her heart on her sleeve for those animals. As he was more than a little bit in love with Rose himself, he could understand. "Is Anna getting any closer to finding a home for all those puppies?" He hoped not. He hadn't had a chance to ask Levi about Rose yet. Hell, he hadn't thought to keep her, not even sure that would work at the compound either, but he didn't want to let her go.

Louise gave him a lopsided grin. "Did you put in your

request for one?"

He chuckled. "It's not that easy. We have to have Levi and Ice's agreement for that," he said with a droll smile. "Just think about it. A lot of us live inside the compound. Just a few of the individual apartments have been constructed on the property. Imagine if puppies lived there inside the compound too."

She nodded. "You shouldn't have just one. It's a huge place. Two would be good to keep each other company."

He nodded. "I figured the women might use their wiles to talk Ice and Levi into keeping one or two." Maybe Rose could be one of those.

Their small talk continued until the meal arrived. Louise stared at the huge bowl of soup with a big slab of French bread on the side, and her stomach growled.

He chuckled.

"This looks lovely." She motioned to the food with an embarrassed smile.

He nodded. "Like I said, the soup and salad here is to die for."

She dug in with joy.

By the time they got back to her clinic, Rory was happy to see Logan pull in behind them.

Logan hopped out and said, "Great. So I get to work while you guys take off for lunch."

Rory grinned. "She didn't eat breakfast."

Logan shot Louise a look that had her flushing.

"Okay. I'll take better care of myself," she said. "You two guys are nags."

Logan chuckled. "I understand the value of regular sustenance for energy. No way could we do the work we do all day long, in all kinds of conditions, if we didn't take care of ourselves."

She nodded. "I hear you." She walked inside, leaving Rory and Logan alone. They unloaded everything Logan had collected. "Stone had most of it waiting for us. Flynn will come by in an hour and give us a hand."

"Excellent," Rory said, and he meant it. "I figured Flynn would help out."

"Definitely. Anna wanted to come too, but she's better off staying with the animals. As much as I appreciate the thought, she doesn't have any experience with security systems."

The next four hours were busy as they worked around the staff and patients. They met dozens of dogs, commiserated with half a dozen cats and even helped a goat inside. The goat was more than interested in Rory's tool belt. By the time the end of the day came, Rory could see just how busy the clinic really was. It was one thing to know it but another to see all the people and animals coming and going. "She sees a lot of animals here."

Logan nodded. "She also handles a lot of large animals. According to Anna, Louise was looking for a large animal vet to come into the practice so she doesn't have to do all of it herself."

"Meaning, horses?"

"Horses, cows, goats, lamas, all kinds of services are needed for them too. Shots, pregnancy testing, etc.," Logan said. "But it is a little hard to entice a large animal vet here. They can get higher wages and easier work in other parts of the country."

"Not to mention a lot of the ranches probably do much of the basic doctoring themselves."

"Good point." Logan looked at him. "Does your brother

do that stuff?"

"We did a lot—only brought in the vet if we had to. Times are changing. No doubt most people prefer to bring in somebody to handle pregnancy testing, and that can take several days, depending on how many head the ranch is running at any time."

With the conversation going on, they were surprised to hear Louise's voice behind them. "How close are you to quitting for the day?"

Rory turned to see her standing behind him, her purse in her hand. He glanced at his watch, surprised to see it was well past six. He looked to Logan. "We've still got another four or five hours at least. Tonight or tomorrow?"

"Might as well do it tomorrow as we're still waiting for a couple more parts to come in," Logan said. "Stone will pick them up in town and bring them here for us once he gets word the delivery has arrived."

Rory straightened and said, "We will shut her down now then. We'll run watches on the place for the next few nights."

Logan looked at Rory. "Are you okay to babysit?"

Louise spluttered. "Nobody is babysitting me," she snapped.

"Oh, hell yeah, he is. If it isn't him, it's me. I figured you'd prefer him," Logan said with an innocent look.

Louise rolled her eyes. "I forgot how cheeky you guys are."

"You are just tired," Rory said. "If we leave now, we can pick up some groceries and cook dinner." He said it in such a matter-of-fact way, as if he hoped she would just agree.

Sure enough she nodded her head, although a little nonplussed.

He grinned. "Can you cook?" he asked.

She shrugged in irritation. "I can. Doesn't mean I will."

"No problem," he said cheerfully. "I am a decent hand in the kitchen. Nowhere near as good as Bailey and Alfred of course, but we won't starve."

She raised both hands in mock surrender. "I'm a decent cook, but I want pasta tonight."

He nodded. "Pasta is good." He considered the concept for a moment. "Do you have the stuff at home?"

She nodded. "I was thinking of a beef stroganoff."

"Now that's perfect."

The two men separated, but Logan called Rory back for a moment. In a low tone he said, "Stone said there's some unusual traffic going back and forth on the main road here. He has seen the same vehicle four times."

Instantly all the lighthearted laughter fell away. "Description?"

"Small red Toyota pickup. The bumper's rusted. Looks to be about a twelve-year-old model. Solo male driver."

"Okay, I will watch out for it."

"Not only watch out for it but plan for it. Chances are he's waiting until the place is empty."

"Okay," Rory growled. "We got it covered." He nodded to Logan and left. Rory motioned to Louise to get into her truck. "If we don't need to hit the grocery store, let's go straight home."

She looked at him suspiciously, then over at Logan and asked, "Why?"

Rory gave her a sweet smile and said, "Because I say so. Now let's go."

She searched his gaze for a long moment and then, without asking any further questions, hopped into her vehicle.

If she gave her truck a little bit too much gas as she raced out of the parking lot, he put it down to temper. He was okay with that. He liked a little bit of spirit in women, and she had a decent amount. Especially when riled. That just made it all the more fun to poke her.

His eyes searched the road for other drivers as he drove behind her. The last thing they wanted was to have somebody follow her home.

Chapter 6

DINNER WAS A fun lighthearted affair. Rory was good company. She hadn't realized just how nice it was to have somebody in the kitchen cooking with her. In an odd way they shared the space very well. She didn't know if it was because he was better housetrained than a lot of the men she knew or because he enjoyed cooking. If he chopped onions, she sliced the meat, and, if she got the pasta from the cupboard, he was already putting the pan full of hot salted water on the stove. She made a comment about it, and he just laughed.

"I like cooking," he said. "I don't do much at the compound because of Alfred."

"And Bailey?"

Rory chuckled. "Yes, Bailey is in the kitchen as often as she can be. Between the two of them, they work well. But then Alfred's of an age where he looks at Bailey almost like a daughter."

"That's probably not a bad relationship to have," she admitted. "My parents are back east. They live in one of those retirement centers for people fifty and over. They love it. A lot of times they don't have to cook because there are so many potlucks and social gatherings and barbecues." She chuckled. "Not necessarily what I want for my life right now."

"It would be hard for you. Although I guess, if you eased up your workload, there might be some energy left for a social life."

"I hadn't really thought about how antisocial I'd become until I contemplated what life for everyone at Levi's place must be like," she said. "There are so many people living there, and most are around the same age."

"I hadn't either until I arrived at the compound. I just came from the better part of a year at the family ranch where the only social life I had was introducing animals in heat to their herd sire."

At that she laughed. "Good for them but not so much for you."

He gave her a droll look. "Isn't that the truth?"

Before long they had their plates full of hot simmering beef stroganoff. He studied his meal in front of him. "I usually put red wine in my stroganoff."

She nodded. "I would if I had any, but I don't."

He frowned. "We should have stopped at the liquor store."

"I don't think that was on top of our minds."

"No, I was trying to make sure you weren't followed home."

"And I was trying to make sure you were watching how I wasn't being followed home," she said, chuckling. She took a bite and closed her eyes in delight. "Now this is tasty." She glanced at him to see if he agreed. From the look of rapture on his face, she figured that, between them, they'd done just fine.

He had such a look of joy as he opened his mouth and popped in the second bite.

She laughed. "Obviously food is important to you."

"Food, companionship and, of course, sex."

She rolled her eyes at the last bit.

He grinned. "It makes the world go around."

"It does indeed," she said.

They polished off dinner at a decent but reasonable pace. When Louise pushed away her empty plate, she sat back with a happy sigh. "That was delicious."

He nodded, looked over at the pot still on the stove and then back at her with a raised eyebrow.

She nodded. "Help yourself."

He hopped to his feet and refilled his plate. She watched in awe as he inhaled that serving too. "I don't know how you guys do it," she said. "And it's not just you. I've seen the amount of food Alfred and Bailey prepare. Every one of you guys is a big eater."

He shrugged. "We work hard. Have to have the fuel when we need it."

She glanced into the kitchen. With the two of them working so well together, very few dishes remained to be cleaned up. As she'd been serving, he'd already filled the sink with hot soapy water and had done all the prep dishes. "You're very good in the kitchen."

"Don't tell Alfred and Bailey that," he said with a wicked grin.

She shook her head. "Although I'm sure they could use the help, they make it all look so effortless."

"That's part of the joy of being there. Everybody knows what their job is, and they do it. So it all seems effortless." He pushed his plate back and said, "That was an excellent meal." Just then his cell phone rang.

She stilled and waited for him to answer it.

With his gaze on hers, he said, "Levi, what's up?"

Immediately she knew something was wrong.

"Did the second vehicle stop? Did we get a license plate or any description of the driver? Who was on watch?"

She crossed her arms over her chest, listening.

"Flynn?" Rory's face relaxed. "So chances are somebody came to check it out and then realized the place was under security. We'll have to watch for that. If they're desperate enough, they'll come back tonight with somebody else." He nodded. "Yeah, I'll tell her." He hung up and said, "You probably heard most of that, but there's been some traffic at your place."

"Anybody hurt?"

"No. Flynn was on watch. They must've been spooked over something. A guy drove up to the building, did a full circle around and then pulled out his phone. He decided against approaching."

"Do you think somebody else will join him?"

"No way to tell, unfortunately. It's possible though."

She nodded. "So can we relax, or do you think we need to go there?"

"We can relax. Flynn's on it. Levi is sending one of the other guys over too. The first guy could be coming back with somebody who has better electronics training than he has. It's obvious we were working on the security system today."

She nodded. "I remember the wires everywhere."

"We couldn't finish the job today, so it's still being set up. Whether they understand that or not, it's hard to say."

She inspected her hands, not surprised to find them trembling.

He reached across, grabbed one and said, "It's fine. It will be fine."

"I'm not so sure about that. I wish there was a way to let

them know I don't have the drugs anymore."

"What do you want to do? Post a sign on the clinic door?" he asked in a half-joking voice.

She looked at him and said, "Yes, I do actually. I mean, if these guys are coming around and looking for that case of drugs, then they need to know I don't have it anymore."

"But, as these guys couldn't have missed seeing the sheriff's deputy's marked vehicle here for over ninety minutes this afternoon, it makes sense that they're spooked now."

She frowned. "It's a little distressing to think the clinic is still one of their targets whether the drugs are there or not."

"I agree." He checked his watch. "You have patients you need to check on tonight."

She frowned at him. "Yes, how do you know that?"

He gave her a lopsided grin. "I've worked on a ranch for a long time. Lived and worked on a ranch," he corrected. "So I do understand animals and watched those two dogs come in today."

She nodded. "One is under observation before surgery. The other came from another clinic. The owners were upset at his care and brought him in. I have to admit that he's not in great shape. So I need to go back and check on him." She glanced at her watch. "Not just yet though. If we check around eleven, I can return in three or four hours, depending on how they're doing."

"Do you ever stay at the clinic overnight?"

Something in his tone made her glance at him sharply. "Yes, there's a cot in my office, and I've used it many times."

He nodded. "That's what I figured. Let's hope it's not required tonight."

She shrugged. "I will if I think I need to."

He shook his head.

She reached over and squeezed his hand. In a firm voice she repeated, "I will if I need to."

He frowned at her.

"Don't bother telling me that I can't or I shouldn't because I will. If the animals need me, I'm staying."

"Are there two cots in your office?"

She stared at him for a moment and then realized he would stay with her. She shook her head. "No. You wouldn't have to stay with me."

"Don't even go there," he warned. "Until this is over, I'm attached to your side."

She raised both hands in frustration. "Until what's over? Do you realize how long that could take?"

"I do. But I also can't take the chance of these guys grabbing you to find their drugs. So protection detail it is. For however long it takes."

"What do you think they'd do?" Inside her stomach churned at the idea.

He gave her a look. "You know what they'd do."

She really didn't want any details. "There's only so much I can deal with right now, and worrying about being kidnapped and tortured is not one of them." She stood and said, "You did all the cleaning up of the prep dishes. I'll finish." She gathered the plates and washed them up quickly so he couldn't step in and do it for her.

When he didn't, she was somewhat surprised. As she turned around, she found him in front of her living room window, talking on the phone. She realized he'd taken advantage of her being so busy to make a few plans of his own. No point in being pissed at him because he was doing exactly what he was supposed to do. Protect her.

She just didn't know how she felt about having somebody that close to her. He was easy to get along with and fun to have around. But he wasn't a habit she should become accustomed to. Because this was one habit she wouldn't get to keep.

RORY LOOKED UP from his work and studied Louise. She was buried in some files she had brought home with her. "When do you want to go?"

She didn't appear to hear him. Or maybe she was just working hard on something she needed to finish.

He turned his attention back to his own work. He was going over her security system, contemplating a few more tweaks and upgrades. It would cost a little more but not much, and it would make a big difference in terms of expanding things later.

The house was clean; leftovers were put away; the dishes were done, and they'd been working on their own things for at least an hour. It was about eleven o'clock, which was when she said she wanted to check on her animals. A few minutes later, he looked up again and said, "Louise?"

She lifted her head. "Yes?"

"When do you want to go to the clinic?"

She glanced at her watch. "Oh, I didn't realize it was so late."

He smiled. "It's not a good habit to bring work home."

She gave a half snort. "You're a fine one to talk."

He nodded. "I know, right? At least it's your security system I'm working on."

She dropped the files back into the folder she brought with her to take a look at his preliminary scratchings on a notepad. She started to ask a question, then stopped and shook her head. "I probably won't understand it anyway. So, as long as you guys figure it out, and you know what to do, then I'm good."

He chuckled. "Let's go." He shut down his laptop, placed his scratch pad on top and considered whether he should take it with him. He hated to. It was a quick trip, but he'd learned the hard way that quick trips weren't always quick. Often they needed a whole lot more work and effort than he had originally thought. Maybe he should consider that this time too. He packed up his computer bag, and, with that in one hand, he picked up his keys and waited at the front door. She joined him a few minutes later. She glanced at the keys in his hand and said, "Are you okay to drive?"

"Of course. Why wouldn't I be?"

She shrugged. "I just figured I should drive."

He shook his head. "It might be better if no one sees you or your vehicle."

She froze for a mere second, then nodded. "If you say so."

With both of them seated in his truck, he drove to the clinic. As they pulled into the parking lot, he sent a text to Flynn. **We're here to check on the animals.**

Good. No action in the last hour.

Rory put away his phone. "Nothing's happened here since you left."

Relief swept across her face. "That's great." She hopped out of the truck and walked up to the front door.

He rushed up behind her and said, "Let me." He undid the rigged system and let her in.

"I guess it might be a bigger trap with my security system unfinished rather than finished, as you're the only one who knows how to disarm it," she said with a half laugh.

He smiled as he quickly hooked the wires back up again. She didn't stay to watch. She headed straight to the back. Instead of following her, he took a moment to walk through the place, checking all the wires and boxes they'd set up. It was a simple system, but he didn't look forward to redoing all the work just because some asshole had crept in and undone it all. After Rory was satisfied everything was as it should be, he joined her in the animal area of the surgery room. Cages of all different sizes were stacked on top of each other.

He found Louise with a gray-multicolored tabby in her arms. He sported a shaved spot on his abdomen and had tubes coming out. Yet the cat's huge purring engine worked just fine and the cat had a look of ecstasy in his eyes. Rory reached over but hesitated, then looked at Louise and asked, "May I?"

She nodded and smiled. "This guy would be forever grateful."

For several long moments, they cuddled the cat. His engine never slowed. When Louise took a step toward the cage, Rory watched as she carefully placed the cat back inside and made sure his lines were clear and then locked him up. She made a notation on the clipboard outside.

"Isn't the clipboard a bit old tech?"

"Sure is," she said cheerfully. "These notes will be transferred to the computer files later. But, for the moment, it's a good system for letting people know when he was last checked."

She went through a couple cages, stopping for a moment to talk to different animals. He saw the respect and love on her face as she handled each one. After a lifetime with animals, Rory appreciated her and her manner toward them. "You really love your job, don't you?"

"Every part of the job except for when I have to put down an animal. Sometimes it's a kindness if they are too sick or too injured, but often it's just because of one difficulty or another. If we had better technology and better medicine, they could be saved, but too often there's nothing we can do."

He understood. He'd seen it over and over again on the ranch too.

When she was finally done, she looked around and said, "The first shift comes in at six."

"Do we need to come back?"

She shook her head. "No, the animals are doing fine. We can go home and go to bed now." As soon as those words were out, a flush walked up her neck and cheeks.

He grinned, but he didn't say anything. She was embarrassed enough. He followed her back out to the front door and saw headlights sweep down from the highway. He watched as they went past the parking lot. When they did, he could hear her slowly let out her breath. He glanced at her and smiled. "Not everybody is coming here to do you harm."

"No, but just having that one was one too many." She stepped into the parking lot and walked over to his truck. He followed after reconnecting the temporary system he'd put together. Outside again, he pulled out his phone. He texted Flynn. **Heading home.**

Okay, check in when you're there came the answer.

They made it onto the road, headlights shining bright in front of them. When she yelled, "Stop," he hit the brakes. They were just at the edge of the clinic property. She pointed ahead to something lying on the side of the road. Cautiously he drove closer. It would be the perfect opportunity for a trap. He pulled up beside it. Before he had a chance to stop her, she jumped from the truck and raced forward. It was an animal of some kind. She checked it over and then came running back. "It's an injured dog. He's been hit but is still alive. I need to get him back to the clinic."

Rory hopped out, took a look and saw the dog was too big for her to lift. Using his spare work shirt stowed in his truck, he gently wrapped up the poor thing, who even now struggled to get away. Covering him, Rory lifted him to put him into the bed of the truck, but Louise already sat in the driver's seat and said, "Come on. I'll drive."

Considering that was the easiest way to go, he took the passenger seat, holding the dog gently. It whimpered in his arms, damn near breaking his heart. He studied the area, wondering what happened, and how long the animal had lain there. He could swear the dog hadn't been there when they arrived. He wondered how long it would take her to realize that fact. Awkwardly she turned the truck around and then drove back to the clinic.

"I don't know if you can disarm the security system while you have him in your arms, but I need him in the back room."

He couldn't do anything while carrying the dog. Once they arrived, she dropped the tailgate, and he gently laid the dog down. Then he uncoupled the wires so they could get back inside. He scooped up the dog and carried him through to the large surgery area.

She tapped a large stretcher. "Put him on here please."

He gently laid the dog down. Within seconds, she had his old shirt pulled away and the dog stretched out. She tugged on gloves and said, "I need to check him over."

"I'll lock up the truck. Be right back." He ran out to the truck, closed his passenger door and the tailgate, and headed back inside, resetting the security on the way. Just as he finished, his phone rang. It was Flynn.

"What's up?" he asked.

"We found an injured dog on the side of the road. Just where you saw us stop."

"The vehicle here earlier stopped there briefly and then carried on."

"Of course it did," he said. "Either they hit the dog by accident or dropped off the dog as a way to lure her back here."

Flynn said, "I wouldn't be at all surprised. Keep a watch on her in there."

"You keep a watch out there," Rory said. "Text every ten minutes if all is well so I get the buzz and know everything's cool."

"Will do."

Rory put his phone on vibrate so he could feel it in his pocket. Then he headed back to where Louise worked. He washed his hands and approached. "What can I do to help?" he asked.

She looked up at him gratefully. "I don't know how long he's been lying there, but he has several cracked ribs, and his front leg is broken."

"Do you have an X-ray machine?"

She was already wheeling the dog into a small room. "Can you help me realign him?"

Under her instructions, the dog was laid out the way she wanted him. Rory didn't like the look of the dog's front leg, but she had an IV in him, and the dog appeared to be calm. Whether she'd given him antibiotics or an anesthetic, he didn't know, but the dog wasn't fighting his rescuers. Maybe he just understood he was in good hands.

With the X-rays developed, Louise pushed them into place in the reader and pointed to the front leg. "It looks like he's been hit by a car. The front leg's got a clean break, and he took a heavy blow to the front shoulder and chest. The shoulder has soft tissue damage, but that will heal on its own. Looks like the vehicle clipped a couple ribs too."

She checked the alignment against the X-ray and then quickly casted it. "The ribs," she said, "are cracked but will heal without any intervention from me as long as he stays calm. He's a young dog and will bounce back fairly quickly. He's in decent shape otherwise. Still it's lucky we found him."

"Would he have lasted the night?"

She nodded. "But in a great deal of pain. He was likely unconscious, only coming around before we arrived."

By the time she and her patient settled for the night, another hour had gone by. In fact, it was almost one o'clock in the morning. "Are you ready to go home?"

She frowned and stared at the patient. "Was it deliberate, do you think?"

He winced. "I was hoping you wouldn't consider that."

She shot him a hot look. "That vehicle that went ahead of us?"

He nodded. "It's possible. You tell me though. I didn't see the dog when we came down here, and we weren't here very long. Could the injuries have been that fresh?"

She nodded. "They were very fresh."

"There's your answer then."

Chapter 7

"**D**O YOU THINK it was meant to lure me here? Or was done out of revenge?"

"Hard to say. I don't want to get hung up on that. The bottom line is, it takes some kind of an asshole to do something like this."

"You're not kidding," she said. "He shouldn't be allowed to get away with that."

Rory nodded. "Give us a chance to catch him."

"Is it safe to go home?"

"I suspect they're watching us," he commented.

A creepy sensation crawled over her skin. "Meaning?"

He shrugged. "Meaning, if this was a set up, they could be preparing to attack. That or they'll try to follow you home."

"Now that they know about your truck?"

"Doesn't matter if they do or not," he said. "Now they know you aren't alone."

She glanced around and said, "Maybe we shouldn't leave then."

"What do you think they will do?"

She turned to look at him, determination in her gaze. "If they're actually running down animals to bring me here, maybe we should make sure I am here." She could feel her stomach knot at the thought of somebody deliberately hurting an animal. "I can't have more animals hurt because of me."

"It's not very comfortable here," he warned. "We could be staying all night for nothing."

She raised her eyebrows. "I don't really care about comfort. I care about them not hurting anybody else." She waved a hand toward the surgery room and the dog she now had safely in a cage. "What if they come back and hurt these guys?" She narrowed her gaze. "Why don't you drive away? Lead them off. Get some of the guys to help, and maybe you can catch these assholes. I will stay here and guard the animals."

"Lead them away and leave you here?" He stared at her in shock, then shook his head. "Not happening."

She frowned at him in frustration. "It's a perfect opportunity to set a trap for them. Flynn is outside somewhere, right?"

He nodded. "That's true, but I need more people than just me and Flynn. We need somebody to drive my vehicle away and somebody else to remain here inside with you. And somebody outside."

She snorted. "That's three men. Is that practical?"

"Somebody has to stay with you at all times." He pulled out his phone and called Flynn.

She walked away to look at each of the animals. Inside her stomach still churned. She couldn't let anything intentionally happen to her animals or her staff either, and neither did she want to die herself. She needed these men to catch this guy. Right now was a perfect opportunity, if they would act on it. She heard a sharp exclamation and turned.

"You stay here," Rory said, pointing a finger at her. "A vehicle is turning into the parking lot."

She froze and nodded. Urgently she said, "Go."

He raced forward, pulling a weapon from under his T-shirt at the back of his jeans. She hadn't even realized he'd been carrying one. She didn't know what she was supposed to do. She walked over and shut off all the lights. If somebody was coming in, she wouldn't make it easy for them. As an afterthought, she reached for a scalpel and popped it into her pocket. She might not have a gun, but she was extremely handy with a knife.

She walked into her office, from where she could see the road, and watched as headlights turned toward the building. The vehicle drove very slowly. The driver had to have seen Rory's truck, had to know someone was here. Just then, the lights on the vehicle were killed, but she could still hear the engine approaching. She walked out to the reception area to find Rory standing beside the big front window.

He pointed a finger at her and said, "Stop there. I don't want them to see you."

She nodded and retreated to the surgery area where she had a view of the action. She also had a hell of a lot of weapons here. Ones she knew how to use. She pulled up a chair close to the cage holding the dog she'd found tonight and sat in the darkness.

And waited.

The trouble with waiting in the dark like that was her mind created a bogeyman at every corner. She found herself shrinking into the chair as if expecting somebody to burst in at any moment. She wanted to send Rory a text. Ask if everything was okay, but she was too afraid she would alert the intruder to where he was with a ping of his phone. She didn't want whoever was in that vehicle to actually gain access to the clinic.

Surely, with both Rory and Flynn here, she'd be safe. But the longer the silence went on, the more her heart slammed against her chest, and the more she could barely breathe.

When one of the dogs beside her yipped, she almost fell off her chair in fear. She was just like an elastic band, stretched so tight she was ready to spring forward. She took several steps, tapping her chest lightly, trying to calm down. She wished somebody would say something. Just as she was about to sit down again, she heard an odd spitting sound, followed by a crack of a window and the sound of shattered glass.

She froze. What the hell was that? Her nostrils flared. She tilted her head slightly, sniffing the air—and catching a whiff of gas. She raced to the surgery doors and hit the lock. As part of the renovations she'd completed after purchasing the clinic, she'd deliberately put in sliding glass doors with a seal and locks to go along with a decent filtration system. The animals were safe inside with her. She walked over to the control panel.

The air-conditioning system hummed as it brought fresh air inside and circulated around the room. With any luck they'd be safe until the men could take these guys down.

An arm slammed against the glass door. A muffled cry escaped. She slapped her hand over her mouth as she stared at the frosted glass. He didn't slam again, and her cell phone didn't go off with a message saying it was safe to come out. She worried about Rory. He'd have told her not to bother, that he could look after himself. But she wasn't so damn sure. She was afraid that had been some kind of smoke bomb or tear gas and wondered what was going on out there. She didn't have Logan's number, but she did have Ice's and

Levi's.

She quickly sent Ice a text, warning her something had happened and about the potential gas. And that she'd had no contact with either Flynn or Rory. Her response was immediate: **Stay where you are. Don't move.**

Louise texted back what she'd done—locking herself into the surgery area with fresh air flowing to keep the animals safe. She warned Ice that gas was in the main part of the clinic. Ice's response read **We're on the way.**

Pocketing her cell phone, Louise slipped back against the cages and stared at the sliding doors. The frosted glass wasn't intended to keep intruders out. It created a vacuum-sealed door for the HVAC system she had put in specifically for this surgery area. Bone dust and animal odors could be potent over time. Not in the interests of anyone's best health to inhale either. This surgery area had no windows. The system was intended to send the air and dust up through the HVAC system, filter it twice before expelling it outside—not into the reception area.

By the same token all the supply cabinets and medicines were behind her in case of breakage. Those fumes, individually or collectively, could be toxic in great quantities. As far as she could see in the darkness through frosted glass doors, everything looked the same as it had been. If somebody wanted to get in, they'd have to come through the opaque sliding glass surgery doors.

It wasn't the best layout. Normally this area was open so nurses had easy access to what they needed to refill the trays for surgery and to bring in patients throughout the day. It was a busy part of the clinic. She did surgeries two days a week, and, during those times, the back of the clinic was a well-oiled system.

Just as she started to relax, the door rattled. Somebody was playing with the lock. She shifted against the rear wall. She didn't know who the hell was there, but they hadn't exactly called out to see if she was okay. With a scalpel in her hand, she sidled up beside the door and waited.

RORY WASN'T EXPECTING the gas canister when it smashed through the window. For some reason that thought had never crossed his mind. Maybe it was because animals were in here, and he would never have endangered them. Or maybe he hadn't realized the level of the people involved in this drug business.

Now that he knew, well, that was an entirely different story. The gas canister had already released the bulk of its gas, but not before he managed to pick it up and toss it back out again. All that really did was let the people outside know he was in here, alive and still conscious.

He was good with that, and, with his T-shirt pulled over his face, he was already on the move. Unless they were perfectly aware of the inside layout, he still had the advantage. He crept toward the surgery doors. A couple rooms were between them, but he needed to make sure nobody got to Louise.

He'd already texted Flynn, warning him about the gas. Hopefully somebody from Levi's compound was coming too. He'd heard two different voices. There was always a chance a third man, a silent one, lurked in the shadows.

When they came through the security system on the front door, the wires he'd put together separated. A bell went off in the background. But it wasn't horrific. He could hear them talking, but they were too far away to actually understand their words. When he heard them laugh, he realized they understood the security system was a bit of a joke. And they were right. That was because the damn thing wasn't finished yet. The men spread out, searching the clinic. Rory knew they'd find him pretty soon.

They were also likely to be heading for the drugs. He couldn't allow that to happen. A man came around the corner and, accidently or by luck, turned his back to Rory. He threw his arm around the man's neck, choking off his air as Rory kicked his feet out from under him. As he went down, Rory helped him fall and smashed his head into the floor. The gunman was out cold. With a grim smile, Rory bounced to his feet, checked the man for weapons and pulled out two pistols. He tucked them into his waistband, and, after making sure the man was out cold, he crept forward, looking for the second intruder.

"Mark? Where are you?"

Rory could hear the second man call out again.

"Mark? Where are you?"

When there was no answer, Rory slid to the side and dropped to the floor. His eyes still watered from whatever gas they had used. He struggled to breathe. His T-shirt remained over his mouth, but the gas was taking its toll. The other man didn't wear a gas mask though, so whatever they had used wasn't that toxic. It was probably knock-out drugs more than anything. That would just help the unconscious man stay that way.

Good.

Rory crept over toward the reception area and watched a shadow pass through the first patient room and head toward the main section in the back, where Louise had a large unused room. On the other side of that section was the surgical theater.

That was where Louise should be, but then he didn't trust her to stay put just because he had told her to. He crept through another patient room. It was dark, and he didn't dare turn on a light.

A noise sounded to his right, like the intruder had tripped over a chair and fallen. His arm slammed into the frosted glass doors as he tried to catch himself before going down.

Rory was on him in an instant. Rory grabbed him by the shoulders and shoved him against the wall. Then he dropped him, but the intruder flipped, rolled over and kicked up. Rory saw stars as he took the blow on his jaw. He fell to his knees, bringing his legs up ahead of him, but the asshole was already on him. Still seeing stars and stunned from the gas, the guy was now choking Rory. He shoved his thumbs into the man's eyeballs. Free now, Rory rolled out of the way and bounced to his feet. He was coughing himself now, kicking and punching, twisting, rolling and fighting for dominance. Finally he got a good solid kick into the man's groin, flipped him and, with his right fist, hit him hard in the jaw.

Silently the man's head rolled to the side. He was out.

Rory sat there for a second, gasping for air. Finding it hard to see, but knowing that Louise was on the other side of that glass door, probably unconscious, he struggled to his feet. Outside the door, he dropped to his knees, pulled out his tool kit and picked the lock.

And pushed it open.

"Louise?" he croaked and then coughed, the gases forcibly expelled from his lungs. Instantly he felt her arms around him.

"Come in here," she cried, pulling him forward. "The air

in here is clear."

As soon as he was in, she slammed shut the door and locked it. He lay on the ground, breathing the fresh air that flowed through the filtration system. He opened his eyes and rubbed at them, but Louise grabbed his hands.

"Don't touch them," she said. "I've got something for them." She ran over to a cabinet and came back.

Holding his eyes open, she squeezed some drops into them, and they felt better. He pushed himself up onto his elbows and said, "Are you okay?"

She nodded. "I'm fine. How are you?"

He shrugged. "I'll be okay." They heard vehicles outside.

"Where's Flynn?" she asked with a frown.

Rory shook his head. "I'm not sure. I expected him to arrive anytime. I've got two unconscious men out there, and I need to make sure they stay that way."

She gasped. "Is that our or their reinforcements?"

Just then her phone went off. She answered it. "Ice, we're in the surgery room. I've got Rory here. No sign of Flynn. Two men are down somewhere in the clinic."

"Okay, we've got masks. We're coming in."

"Be careful. We don't know if there is a third man," Rory yelled.

"I heard him," Ice said to Louise. "We've got it covered."

Louise put away her phone and sat beside Rory. "How are your eyes?"

"Better than my throat," he said with a groan.

She got up and poured him a glass of water. "You need to get checked out at the hospital."

He gave her a wry look. "I'd normally be okay with that, but, chances are, we'll have the deputies here soon, and the same nightmare to contend with all over again."

She shook her head. "When will this end?"

"Soon. Very soon." Just then a rap came on the glass door. He could see Ice's face pressed against the frosted glass. Not enough to be clear, but, with her long braid hanging down in front, it was pretty obvious who it was.

Louise unlocked the door, and Ice stepped through, taking several deep breaths of the air. She smiled. "Nice HVAC system."

"It is. I always had a thought at the back of my mind," Louise admitted, "that I could do some specialized work here."

"What kind of work would you need that kind of filtration system for?" Levi asked from behind Ice.

Louise's face lit up when she saw him. "I was looking to do prosthetics for animals," she explained. "A couple clinics in England do some amazing work. But it entails a lot of bone grinding. And in that case—well, bone dust is deadly for so many reasons."

Levi and Ice looked at her in interest. Rory just lay on the floor and smiled. He really liked big thinkers. People with plans. Grinding bones didn't sound like fun, but prosthetics for dogs, cats, horses, … hell yeah. Using one of the benches beside him, he struggled to his feet.

Ice checked him over. "How's your throat?"

"Burning but I'll be fine," he said shortly. "Any sign of Flynn?"

"We have Merk and Logan out looking for him."

"What about the vehicle? Do we know anything?"

"Not yet but we will in a few minutes," she said with a smile. "Harrison's on that right now."

"And the deputies?"

Levi laughed. "On their way. You are allowed to leave something for us to do, you know."

Rory shook his head. "We were actually arguing about whether we should leave or stay."

"What was that about picking up a dog on the road?"

Rory explained what happened. He finished with "I think it was deliberate. Hoping she'd see the animal, bring him back here, so they could return and hit the clinic with her inside."

"Chances are they were already waiting for you then," Levi said. "They just needed time for their reinforcements to get here before you left."

Rory nodded. "That's what I figured too." He turned to look at Louise. "You're sure you don't have anything else here they might want?"

She shrugged. "There's a lot they might want, like the legitimate drugs used for animals. But the only case of that crap of theirs is at the sheriff's office. Only they don't know that, and that's a problem."

"By the time we confiscate their cell phones, and check out who and what these guys are, we should get that message across."

"They didn't come here from some local gang," Rory said. "Not with gas canisters like these."

"Those are actually police-issue tear gas canisters," Levi said. "Unfortunately they can be bought all over the place, even on the internet these days. They're not even military grade."

"Right." Rory stared down at the thing in Ice's hand and frowned. "So that's of no help then."

"Only in that it tells us these guys are serious," Ice added, "and they're not letting this go. I don't know if they were after a full shakedown of the clinic, or they just wanted her. However, if they got her, they'd have gotten what they needed anyway because they'd have tortured her to get the information."

"That would have taken all of two seconds," Louise said drily. "I would have handed that information over immediately."

In the background, they could hear sirens. Rory, still feeling the effects of the gas, started choking again.

Louise came to his side. "He needs to get his lungs checked out at the hospital," she said.

Rory shrugged. "I'll be fine."

Louise snorted. "You can be as tough and macho as you want, but you either go to the hospital or I can help clear your lungs here if you choose to be stubborn."

"If he doesn't want to go to the hospital, that's fine," Ice said. "What have you got for his lungs?"

Rory sat back as the two discussed treatment.

"The only thing he really needs is oxygen …" Louise pulled out a large clear plastic mask. "I use these on the larger animals. It won't fit well but hopefully will do the trick." She handed it to Ice while she hooked it up to the oxygen tanks built into the surgery room.

Ice placed the mask over his face, covering both his nose and mouth. From the size of it, he figured Louise must use it on a damn horse. Within minutes, clean fresh oxygen flowed over his face and into his lungs. He took deep gulping breaths, loving the feeling as the air hit his lungs. As soon as it did, he coughed again. He pulled away the mask to clear his air passages, then put it back on again.

With Louise and Ice standing watch, he was forced to do that several more times as he expelled the bad air from his lungs. At last he took several deep breaths and wasn't overcome with coughing. He smiled and said, "Thank you. I feel much better."

Chapter 8

L OUISE STUDIED RORY'S color. The pink had slowly returned to his cheeks. He was almost back to normal. "You still need to be careful of your lungs for a little while."

"What about my eyes?" he said. "I don't know what those drops were, but they were great. It feels like I need more already though."

She returned to her cabinet and pulled out the eye drops. "They aren't meant for tear gas, but they are certainly some of the best on the market for anything irritating the eye." She held them out to him and said, "Can you put them in yourself?"

He nodded, tilted his head back, putting drops into each eye.

"Those can be used anytime and all day long. Keep the bottle. It might get you through the day."

He looked at her in surprise. "How long will the tear gas effects last?"

She shrugged. "I don't know. I guess it depends on how bad a dose your eyes got. They're very red and sore-looking."

"That's because they are," he said shortly, then faced Ice. "Where are we at so far?"

Ice took his measure and then nodded. "Levi's outside. We have one dead man out there and a second in the parking lot."

Rory frowned. He didn't see a man in the parking lot. Before he had a chance to ask, Ice said, "Flynn took him out. Logan has found Flynn too. He's now out at the wood line looking for accomplices."

"Good," Louise said. "Can we move away from the animals? This unusual nighttime activity isn't good for them."

"Better yet, let's move everyone outside to the fresh air," Ice said. Just then Levi joined the group.

"Levi, maybe you could stay here with Louise, until she's ready to come out. She needs to talk to the sheriff."

Louise looked at Levi, and he looked at her.

She shrugged. "I can do that now." She took a last glance around the room, reassured everything was more or less okay, if a bit messy. Then she walked outside.

"Do you know how lucky we are that it isn't one of the nights the cleaners come?" She shook her head. "I didn't even think about them."

"How often do they come?" Levi asked.

"Twice a week. By rights it should be every day, but I have them come in after surgery days."

"That makes sense."

"Do you have many surgeries planned for today?" Rory asked.

She shook her head. "No, surgery was Wednesday. The cleaners came then. The last surgeries were all fairly minor. That makes it easier. I'm trying not to keep anybody overnight because of the problems right now. I can't completely get away from it. In a certain number of cases we have to keep the animals safe from themselves."

Back outside she took several breaths of fresh air. She'd noticed remnants of the gas as she had walked through the reception area, but it wasn't bad. Still, the fear, the damage, her nerves made staying inside the building a claustrophobic experience. As soon as she gulped in the evening air, she felt a cough coming on. She walked away from the group and coughed several times to clear her lungs. Now if only she could clear these incidences from her memory as easily.

"Are you sure I can't just put up a big sign which reads The Drugs Aren't Here Anymore?" she asked, only half joking.

The two men Rory knocked out were held to the side by the sheriff's deputies. They glared at her. She walked over and asked, "Why do you keep coming back here?"

Neither man said anything.

She shrugged. "If you're looking for that case of drugs, ... I already turned it over to the sheriff."

The men still didn't say anything. She turned to Levi and said, "It doesn't do any good to talk to them, does it?"

"Not usually," he said cheerfully. "Chances are good they'll get killed anyway."

She nodded. "Just like the first three, I suppose." She cast another glance back to see nerves working on both men at that news. "Oh, didn't you know one of your guys came and shot the two men who tried to break in the first time, plus killed the delivery driver. You must realize failure is not an option. Now that you've failed, you're both dead."

Rory stepped up to her, put his arm around her shoulder and said, "Come on. Let's leave them in the sheriff's custody. I doubt anybody can get to them there. Right?"

There was something odd in his tone of voice. She glanced at him sharply but let him lead her away. When they were out of earshot, she said, "Did you mean what you said or were you mocking them?"

"If somebody wants to get at them, they'll get at them.

Lots of people already in the prison system would kill these two men for a pack of cigarettes," he said quietly. "Those two know it. I'm giving them a chance to think about what it is they want to do next. If they cooperate, they might walk out of this alive. Regardless of whether they do or not, the group they're associated with will assume they are a liability now. Just like the other three men, they'll take them out."

She rubbed her face. "Why is there so much killing all of a sudden?"

"It's not all of a sudden," Rory corrected. "It's just touching your life right now."

She wrapped her arms around her chest and said, "I need to rest. But I'm scared to leave the animals."

"The deputies will be here for quite a while. You said there was a cot in your office. Why don't we pull it out? You rest, and one of us will stand guard to make sure nobody bothers you."

She frowned. "How can I sleep? The deputies need to talk to me, and my place is a mess. I don't even know if it's safe to bring people in here tomorrow … today," she said, swiftly correcting herself as she looked at her watch. "And then there's the issue of the broken window when they threw in the gas canister."

"You'll have to get somebody in about the window. It's not one of the main front windows, so nobody'll notice unless you point it out. Obviously the staff will know because somebody has to come in, clean this up and then replace it."

At that she winced. "I wonder if I could get the cleaners to come in early this morning. I don't want the staff to know how much of a problem we've got."

"It's too early to call them, but you might be able to

leave a message."

She pulled out her phone and left a message. Then, just to make sure, she sent a text. She liked the idea of crashing here for a couple hours but not when so many people were around. That just made her feel odd.

"I do need sleep though, if I'm to keep up today. Or is that foolish? Should I be canceling all appointments for the day?"

"Depends if you want anyone to know the clinic was targeted or if you can make it through the day as if everything is normal. If anyone asks, just say you found a window broken when you arrived this morning. However, if you shut down for a broken window, that will make people worry."

Louise could feel her shoulders sag. "In that case," she said, turning to Rory, "if you could be so kind as to keep watch, I'll crash on the cot and see if I can at least grab a few hours. You guys can leave whenever you're done, but I might as well just stay here and start the day. It'll be a long one."

"C'mon. Let's see if the sheriff's deputies need to talk to you right away." Rory walked Louise over to where the two deputies were on their phones. As soon as one got off, he turned to Rory and frowned. Then his gaze landed on Louise, and he held out his hand. "Hi, I met you yesterday or the day before. I'm a little confused about the time frame right now," he said with a half smile. "These midnight callouts can be brutal."

She nodded. "I know exactly how you feel. That's actually what I wanted to talk to you about. I need to have the clinic open later today, if at all possible, but I need some shut-eye in order to do that. I've got a cot in my office. How long will you guys be here?"

He glanced around and said, "We need to get some fingerprinting and forensic work done. The team is on the way, and they'll be at it for hours. If we're lucky, we'll be done by six."

She nodded. "I would really appreciate it if that could happen. I need to get this clinic back up and running again. I have a lot of animals in the back, and people will start wondering."

"I can't promise anything, but we'll do our best." He paused, then said, "I can get your statement later if you want." At her nod, he asked, "So are you staying here, or are you going home?"

She frowned considering the options when Rory said, "You would sleep better in your own bed."

"If I sleep at all. At least here I'm on the spot, if anybody needs me."

He nodded. "Your choice."

She thought about all the nights she'd crashed on the cot and had slept reasonably well. When she was tired, she was tired. Making a fast decision, she said, "I'll take the cot." She walked back inside, sniffing the air experimentally. "Can we eliminate the gas odor?"

Levi said, "We have some large industrial fans, filters and blowers to bring in that can recirculate the air. We'll open all the windows and clear it out as much as possible. It is dissipating at a decent rate, but you're right. The odor is lingering."

She looked at him and asked, "Can I leave it in your hands?"

He nodded. "I've got men sitting around doing nothing. They might as well come and work on this."

She rolled her eyes. "Great, now they'll hate me for that too."

"What else would they hate you for?" Levi protested.

She gave him a sideways glance. "The puppies. They love to hate me because I brought the puppies. Unless you're keeping them, that is." With a half laugh at his sour expression, she turned and walked into her office. There she closed the door, pulled out the cot, grabbed a sweater out of the coat closet and had just stretched out when the door opened. She turned to find Rory. He studied the office carefully, as if looking for any weaknesses. When he was finally satisfied, he turned his gaze on her and said, "Don't you have any blankets?"

She shrugged. "I'm not exactly sure what the hell's around here anymore. I had blankets on the cot, but they're not here now."

"Do you have a washer and dryer? A laundry room? I thought I saw one." He turned back toward the surgery room as if mentally laying out the floor plan.

"Yes, I do actually." She tried to sit up, but he motioned to her.

"Stay down. I will get it."

Not wanting to argue she collapsed back down, her head on the pillow, grateful she had a sweater here. She closed her eyes and fell asleep.

RORY MOVED TOWARD the back room, where he thought he'd seen the laundry area. As he entered, he turned on the light to see floor-to-ceiling cupboards. He opened them up and found all kinds of linens. Choosing a nice soft fluffy blanket from the bottom shelf, he pulled it out. Back in Louise's office, he found her lying on the cot, her eyes closed. Her breathing was slow and even. He unfolded the blanket and laid it gently over her. She never moved.

Unable to help himself, he kissed her on the temple and backed out of the room. He checked that the door was unlocked to make sure he could get back in again, then closed it. He'd keep an eye on her office. Make sure no one tried to sneak in.

Rory walked out to meet Levi and Ice. He stood in the middle of the reception area, where he could see the hall that led to Louise's office. The two walked toward him.

"She's crashed in her office," he explained. "I don't feel comfortable leaving her alone."

Ice nodded.

"How about I stay here?" Rory said. "I'll deal with the authorities and make sure the clinic gets cleaned up— hopefully without waking Louise."

"Several of the crew are coming from the compound," Levi said. "However, someone needs to go to the sheriff's office to get as much information as possible. They should have tracked down the vehicle by now."

Ice added, "I texted Stone. He's running facial recognition. Once we ID the men, we need to find out who their associates are, and we need to know fast. So I'll run command center from here for the next hour or two." Ice glanced at her watch. "At that time, if you guys have done all you can, then you can come back and keep watch. She'll be up by six, I'm sure. In the meantime, we need to get this air circulating as fast as possible."

Just as she stopped speaking, they heard vehicles starting up in the parking lot. The deputies were getting ready to return to the sheriff's office.

"It's a good thing this is all fields and pastures here. If Louise had neighbors watching, they'd wonder what the hell was going on," Rory said.

"The neighbors will notice even if not close by," Levi said. "It's always a mistake to think no one witnessed last night's events. Not to mention there is likely to be some news coverage. But Louise just needs to keep putting one foot in front of the other and not get sidetracked. Ice, make sure to tell her to act like nothing has happened." Levi stepped away, motioning for Rory to follow him.

As much as Rory hated to leave Louise, he knew there was a lot to do. As long as somebody was watching over Louise, that was all that mattered. He walked outside to find the deputies loading up the two prisoners. Rory stepped forward and said, "Do we have any identification on them yet?"

One of the deputies looked at him. "They don't have any ID on them, and they're not volunteering any names."

The other deputy asked, "Why do you want to know right now?"

"So I have names for the gravestones in a couple days," Rory said with a smirk.

The handcuffed guy closest to him looked at him hard. "You can't scare us."

Rory shook his head. "I don't give a damn about scaring you. You're nothing to me. It's your boss I want."

"You won't get him."

"We will. We haven't missed any target we've been after yet." Rory's voice was hard but even. He didn't boast casually. He'd been in the military for a long time. They had done an awful lot of crazy-ass missions where he wondered at the possibility of success, but the stuff they'd pulled off ... Well, he'd learned a lot about going beyond what he'd thought was possible. It also told him so much about what the enemy was capable of doing. The enemy he was used to facing versus the enemy he faced now might have different appearances, use different names, but they were still the same assholes inside, and they made mistakes like everybody else.

"Not to worry," Rory said. "You'll find out soon enough."

He smacked the hood of the county car and walked away. The two deputies got in and pulled out of the parking lot. Just after they turned onto the main road, shots filled the air, and the front windshield of the cruiser exploded.

"Shit!" Rory was already running. When the second shot was fired, he knew he wouldn't be in time. The shots came from the other end of the field, against a thin wooded area. He would just be a target himself. Levi grabbed his arm, and both of them hit the dirt as gunfire peppered the ground in front of them. Rory, his head against the gravel, said, "All four do you think?"

Levi nodded. "Guaranteed." His tone was bitter, angry. He peered over the rocks, trying to pinpoint where the shooters were. With his phone in his hand, he dialed and said, "One possibly two shooters as I spotted two muzzle flashes at the tree line. Eleven o'clock from the nose of the deputies' vehicle. Chances are all four inside the cruiser will be dead. High-powered rifles. Good distance and a wind. Plus shots taken in the dark with the headlights of the deputies' car causing a glare at least or a blind spot at worst. We've got some experienced shooters up there. Rory and I are going after them. You check the vehicle."

He put away his phone. They both raced back to Levi's car, Levi screaming at Rory, "Get in."

Once both of them were inside the vehicle, Levi peeled out onto the road and turned in the opposite direction. Still, as they went forward, Rory ducked down just in case the shooters were looking for more targets. Levi quickly made several turns, coming up behind where the shooters had been. In the distance, they heard more sirens. If they couldn't get ahead of the shooters, there was no way to stop them. Their phones were going nuts. Rory grabbed Levi's as he drove and answered it to find Merk on the other end, yelling, "What the hell is going on?"

Rory filled him in.

"I'll get Stone on the satellite right now."

The phone went dead only to ring again seconds later. Rory answered Ice's call. "Ice, we're both fine. I don't know about anybody in the deputies' vehicle."

"I'm not leaving Louise's side. Flynn is outside. He'll report in as soon as I get off the phone."

Levi yelled, "With your medical training, you might need to go to the crime scene. Can you pull in someone else to stand guard on Louise?"

"I see Flynn racing through the tree line toward the pullout up ahead," Rory told her. He could hear Ice walking in the clinic.

"Logan has pulled up to the cruiser," she said. "He's a damn good medic. And he's not alone." Her voice turned brisk. "I need this line open."

"We'll all be too late to catch the shooters anyway. No way they would have set this up beforehand and not had a place to run to. Exits are always the first thing they map out." And Rory ended the call.

With Levi taking every corner as fast as he could, gravel sprayed behind them. It was a wild chase in the night. But they were chasing two ghosts. Levi had no idea where the shooters' vehicle came from or where it could be going, if they were even in the same vehicle. It would be smarter for the two shooters to have their own cars. Levi was waiting on Stone. When the call finally came through, Stone's terse voice filled the car.

"Take a right one hundred meters ahead."

Levi took the corner at top speed. Following Stone's directions, they continued two miles and took a left. Then they turned off onto what appeared to be a hayfield of some kind. "Keep your eye on them," Levi said to Stone. "And conference with Rory."

Within seconds they pulled up behind the shooters' getaway vehicle. Both doors were open, and the men appeared to have bolted.

Rory's phone rang, and he yelled, "I'm taking the right," and hopped out of Levi's truck, plugging in his earpiece to his cell. He didn't wait for an answer but bolted after his target. Both of these men were armed with rifles. Rory needed to keep out of sight or else he'd be targeted himself. He needed Stone to track these men. It was only because of Stone and the satellite that they could even do that much. Up ahead, Rory caught a movement. He picked up his pace. Trying to control his breathing, he asked, "Stone, is this guy turning left?"

"Yes, in about ten feet, turn left hard."

"How far ahead is he?" he gasped out. His feet hit the ground hard as he pelted forward at top speed.

"One hundred feet and closing. He's failing."

"Good. The asshole is about to meet up with a very pissed-off fist."

"Fifty feet," Stone warned.

"Give me a warning at ten and make sure he's going in the same direction I am."

It was barely seconds later when Stone said, "Ten coming up on the right."

Rory could hear the man to the right beside him. He heard his ragged breathing just as Rory plowed into him, knocked him to the ground and, with all his might, pulled his right fist back and drove it into the man's jaw. He stopped moving after that. Rory sat on the man's chest, gasping for air. A rifle was in the man's hand. Rory kicked it away and held him down, but this asshole wasn't going anywhere. He was knocked out cold.

"Stone, I got him."

"I see that. Sit tight."

That he could do. He rubbed sweat off his forehead. Inside was a roar of triumph. They may not have everyone, but they'd caught this asshole. If nothing else, these two gunmen would face the death penalty for shooting the deputies. What Rory and Levi had to do was make sure this one, and possibly the one Levi had, didn't die before Rory and Levi found out who'd given the orders. Rory was getting damn tired of catching these assholes and watching them be murdered before giving them more information.

"How's Levi doing?"

"About to connect with his target," Stone said. "And he got him. Bit more of a struggle and … he's down. Hold on."

Stone disconnected, presumably to talk to Levi. They would need help getting these assholes back to Levi's vehicle, or Rory would have to carry his guy. As he thought about the distance and the path he'd taken, he winced. But the small guy beneath him was lightweight. Probably didn't weigh more than a hundred and forty. Rory had packed heavier guys. Plus, it would be a whole lot easier to deal with this guy if he was out cold and not struggling against Rory. Awake, the gunman would do his damnedest to get free again.

He picked up the man and tossed him over his shoulder in a fireman's carry, grabbing the rifle and starting back the way he had come. He shuffled the rifle and hooked it over the man's feet. He reinserted his earpiece that got knocked out in the struggle and waited for Stone to call him back.

"You're walking?" Stone asked.

"I figured it was probably easier to deal with the asshole while he was out cold than to argue with him when he was a little more spirited."

"Okay. Keep going back all the way to where you took the right-hand turn. You've got a bit of a way to go yet."

Rory shifted the dead weight on his shoulder and kept the phone line open as he walked. Outside of being full of gunfire and hatred, the evening sky was beautiful. Not to mention the sense of satisfaction he had in knowing he'd actually succeeded in capturing this asshole. Tonight ended up on a good note.

"Are Ice and Louise okay?"

"No word on Louise. Presume she's still sleeping. Ice is pissed. She's taking this as a personal affront. She also has more uniforms coming. Nothing like cop shooters to bring out the entire force."

"Great. So much for keeping this quiet."

"Not happening. Logan will get the clinic cleaned up and back up in operation as fast as we can. This doesn't need to interfere with the building being open for business. The shooting was on the main road, so we should be able to keep the far entrance to the clinic's parking lot open."

"Once we have these two shooters in jail, we might get some answers. If we can keep them alive long enough. And if we can convince them to talk …"

"Don't worry. Now that two of their own deputies have been shot and are possibly dead—I don't have an update on that yet—the sheriff's office will make sure these shooters face their reckoning."

Rory hoped so. So far the gunmen were doing a better job at cleaning up their mistakes than anyone else Rory had seen. And Rory had seen a lot.

Chapter 9

LOUISE WOKE UP with a start. She lay still, figuring out what noise she had heard. It sounded like an air-conditioning system on steroids. She sat up and groaned. Her body ached in places she hadn't felt in a long time, and she realized she was sleeping in her office.

Almost immediately all the memories of the previous night came flooding back. She stood up and slowly walked to the bathroom to wash her face. With that done, she stepped out to face whatever nightmare was going on in the remains of her clinic. She was pleasantly surprised to find Ice standing not very far away from her door and issuing orders. She was yelling over the blowers of some kind of an air-recirculating system. Louise stared at the large machines and shook her head, then sidled up to Ice and said, "What the heck is that?"

Ice gave a start, not realizing Louise had come out of her office. Then Ice smiled and said, "To clean out the air."

"Oh, good. What time is it?" Louise asked, brushing her hair off her forehead. "I must have slept hard. I still feel groggy." Avoiding the big machines, she stepped out to the front of the clinic with Ice at her side.

"At least out here we can talk," Ice said with a laugh.

Louise looked around, delighted to see the deputies were gone and no crime scene tape or anything else filled the early morning light. "So once these machines are gone, the clinic can operate again?"

Ice nodded. "There wasn't much left in the way of gas particles. They do dissipate fairly quickly, but this is just to make sure everybody's good. We don't want anything to hurt the animals."

Louise smiled. "It's nice to know you guys are animal lovers too."

"All of us are," Ice admitted. "Bringing in those puppies was a bad idea."

Louise chuckled. "Right. I'm sure you guys are keeping two at least."

Ice shook her head. "Levi's pretty resistant to the idea," she admitted. "Not because he doesn't love puppies, but he figures it'll be nothing but trouble with everybody there. We don't want the dogs playing favorites."

"They will play favorites, and they will bond with whoever loves them. ... They'll probably end up being closest to Alfred. He'll be the one in charge of food."

"Which also means Bailey," Ice said. "And she's already a big softie."

"I think you all are, in your own way," Louise said, following Ice outside to the parking lot. "Any update on the rest of this mess?"

Then she realized Levi's men and more deputies plus policemen swarmed the main road. She stopped and stared. "What happened here?"

In a sober voice Ice quickly brought Louise up to speed.

Louise shook her head. "Oh, my God, both the prisoners and the deputies?"

"The two deputies are alive, but one's in bad shape. We are not sure if he'll pull through. He's in surgery right now.

The other one is in the emergency room. He took a hit high on his shoulder and one to the chest that missed his vitals. Another one grazed his ribs and did some damage, but he'll live."

"And the two intruders?" Louise asked. But inside she knew. They'd been the targets in the first place.

Ice shook her head. "They're both dead. On the other hand, Levi and Rory caught the two shooters."

Louise stared at her in shock. "How did I sleep through all this?"

"It's a good thing you did," Ice said with a laugh. "We had quite some chaos for a while. We've got the two shooters. Our guys are taking them straight to lockup. They have an armed police escort. Once you start shooting cops, everybody gets in on the act."

Louise shook her head. "I tried to warn the intruders, and they just glared at me."

"These types know what they are doing when they get into the drug business," Ice said quietly. "That's small comfort for their families, I know. But how do you put the fear of God into a criminal by telling him that his life will end in disaster when he already knows it? They almost become fatalistic about it. It's as if they don't see any other way."

That made some sense to Louise under those circumstances, but it was still very sad. She deliberately turned her back on all the chaos. "I suppose now the authorities will be working there all day?"

"Possibly. It doesn't necessarily stop access to the clinic. Your customers will know there was a shooting, but nobody will understand what it was about."

"Well, they will eventually. But hopefully by then, everything here will be back to normal." She walked around to see the broken window was boarded up. The curtains could be closed inside to hide that. The rest of the building looked to be normal. Some of the ground was churned up a bit, but it looked fairly decent.

As they stood outside talking, the men with the big equipment inside started to pull out. As they loaded up the industrial fans, they came over to Ice and said, "It looks good in there. Readings are within normal range now."

The two women walked back inside with Louise smelling the air and smiling. "It smells fresh now."

"Not bad, huh?"

Louise checked her watch. It was almost seven. "My staff will be here in half an hour." She shook her head. "On top of that, I didn't check on the animals. So much chaos and then I just crashed. I have to go deal with them now." She stopped and looked at the coffeepot and then turned back to Ice and said, "I don't suppose you know how to make a pot of coffee?"

Ice shooed her away and said, "I've got it covered."

Just then the cleaners arrived. Louise told them what to focus on; then she walked to where the animals were. The air in there smelled fine. She was grateful. The last thing she wanted was any of the animals to have any lingering symptoms from the tear gas. She did have eye drops if needed. As she checked each of the animals over, she took care to inspect their eyes. For a couple of them, she added drops just because they looked dry and sore. By the time she was done, it was almost eight o'clock.

She was no longer alone in the back. Nancy showed up and so did Alice, one of the girls who came in on Fridays to clean the cages. After giving Alice instructions for the day,

Louise headed to the front with Nancy.

"How busy a day is it?"

"Full," Nancy replied. "You'll be here until three, then house calls."

It couldn't be helped. She picked up a stack of files. Before going into her office, she walked to the front door and stepped out. Ice sat in her car, talking on the phone with a laptop on her knees. Shifting the files into her other hand, Louise rapped on the window. Ice closed off the phone call, opened the window and said, "I'm not leaving. I'm just here for a while until we can get somebody else in."

"Do you think we need somebody here all day?" Louise asked, nodding toward the organized chaos on the road. "Surely no one will try again with that police presence."

"Someone will be here until we get to the bottom of this. Logan is returning to work on the security system as well."

"And Rory? Is he okay?"

Ice nodded. "He's at the police station right now. Then he needs to crash for a few hours. He'll return, probably in the early afternoon."

With a smile Louise headed inside to get started on her day. It would be a long one. Her stomach growled. She checked her desk drawers for any granola bars. She found a packet of peanuts from some ancient time. Still, it was food. She popped them down as she went through the folders. Before she had gotten through the first two, the buzzer rang.

Her day had started. She grabbed the first folder and headed off to the waiting room.

There she called out for Mrs. Robinson to bring in her Pekinese. Little Charlie had had his leg amputated over a year ago, but the stump kept giving him trouble. It was another reason why Louise was looking at doing prosthetics for animals. There was such a need, and so few facilities or veterinarians were available to effectively treat these animals. Charlie kept using his stump to move forward in life, and what he really needed was at least a wooden peg to keep him going. She'd looked into getting prosthetics elsewhere and shipping them, but the fitting process itself took time. Still, Charlie would be a good test subject.

As she gave him a thorough examination, his owner looked up and said, "Can we do the metal leg prosthetic like you were suggesting?"

"Possibly. I'm working on some adjustments in the clinic here, so I can start creating some simple ones. We will have to get forms made, have the prosthetics made up and brought back. But I think it's doable."

She bandaged Charlie's stump, put a rubber stopper over the end to give him a little bit more protection and sent him on his way. That was just the start of her day. By the time she'd worked through the morning patients and checked in on the dog she'd found on the road, and happy to see his progress, she returned to her desk at noon. That's when she considered her absolute lack of food here.

At times some of the women had lunches left. And how sad was that when the doctor herself didn't have food. But it seemed like regular meals weren't much of a habit with her. As she walked into the staff room to see if any leftovers remained in the fridge, she heard a familiar male voice out in the waiting room. It was Rory.

"Does she have time to see me?"

Louise stepped into the doorway and said, "Hi, Rory. How are you doing?"

He flashed her a bright smile, holding a box of something.

She could smell it coming as he approached. She rolled her eyes at him but led him back to her office. He stepped through, and she closed the door behind him. "I sure hope that's Chinese food because I'm starved."

"I figured you didn't have any breakfast, and you probably didn't have any lunch. I was taking a chance you weren't going out though, and I'd miss you completely."

"I haven't had a chance to go anywhere." She turned toward him, happy to see no aftereffects from the tear gas. "I hear you had an exciting morning while I slept," she said drily.

"I did indeed. At least you got some sleep, and now, after four hours downtime, I have too. So let's sit down and eat. I can bring you up to speed on everything that's happened." She cleared off a space on her desk, and he handed her a couple take-out boxes.

He looked over and said, "Do you have any plates? I never thought to bring any. If you don't, that's fine. We can just eat from the containers."

She didn't want to take the time to check the back room. So, with two forks, they just split everything half and half, and plowed their way through.

By the time her first wave of hunger was appeased, she sat back with a happy sigh and said, "You were just in time. I was about to beg the ladies for any spare lunch they wouldn't mind sharing."

He grinned and said, "Not to worry. I've got your back."

RORY SHIFTED EVER-SO-SLIGHTLY in the chair. He'd only woken up less than an hour ago, and he'd bolted over with a quick detour to pick up food. When he arrived, he was afraid he was too late, and maybe she'd already gone out. While they worked their way through chicken chop suey, he brought her up to date. "The men are in isolation at the moment in the local jail. They're being treated as top security, in case somebody else comes along to take them out."

"But of course they're not talking yet, correct?"

He nodded. "They're smug, thinking they're at the top of the food chain. Of course they're not, but they haven't quite realized that yet."

"Nobody at the top of the food chain does the actual killing," she scoffed. "They hire it out." She took another bite. "Did they kill the first two men at the clinic?"

He shrugged. "We're not sure yet. But it's possible."

"Possible but not necessarily so. This is just a gang, right? Or a drug cartel of some kind?"

"Something like that. If it's a cartel, it's a pretty small arm of it. What we need to do is get to the manufacturing side behind all this. Take all the drugs off the street and put the business people operating all this behind bars."

"At this rate, they'll take out their own people and then move back across the border."

"*If* they came from across the border. Being here near Houston, we tend to make that assumption, but it's not necessarily true. The US drug trade is alive and well. Plus manufacturing is more viable here in the States as there's no risk crossing any border."

"It's a sad state of affairs," she said. She stole a large piece of meat off one of the other dishes. "This is excellent Chinese food. Thank you. I was hoping for a sandwich at the most, but this is way better."

He chuckled. "At least it's hot, and it's freshly cooked.

And it does get some vegetables in you."

They ate in silence for a long moment as each contemplated the crazy night they'd had.

"So what's next?" she asked.

"First, we finish lunch. Then I'll help Logan complete the security system."

"Can you finish it today? Will it be safe to leave the animals in the clinic overnight without a guard inside?"

"It will be as much as anyplace," he said cheerfully. "The cops need to talk to these gunmen and see what they have to say. And somebody needs to let their boss man know the sheriff has their drugs. Otherwise this won't stop until they've torched the place."

Her face paled as if it was the first time she'd contemplated such an option. Then she swallowed hard and sat back. "I guess that would be an easy answer for them, wouldn't it? If they can't have the drugs, then they destroy the place, and nobody else gets their drugs."

He was sorry he had brought it up, but he had never been one to put his head in the sand. The reality was, she was up against some pretty shitty people. It was just her bad luck she'd ended up in this situation, but it was still the reality she had to deal with, and there was no getting away from that. "We're hoping the men have a lawyer called in. Then some information can be passed to the lawyer. Maybe they'll have an idea of a way forward."

"Are you saying you actually trust lawyers?" she asked in surprise.

He shook his head. "They're not all bad. In this case, we won't make a deal. However, if they find out the drugs are in custody during the interrogation, that'll filter back to the boss man. Once they know that, they should leave your clinic alone."

"That makes sense."

He glanced at his watch and said, "They should be interrogating them right now. What we have to do is make sure they stay alive long enough to talk. If these guys die, then we've lost our last-known connection to the group."

"How many men could they possibly have? They've already killed five of their underlings. Plus Flynn got two of them that they would have shot themselves anyway. So seven died just this week."

"They've got hundreds if they need them. Any number of men are ready to do the job for the right price."

She sank back into her big comfy chair and continued to eat.

He was glad to see her eating this much. Normally she ate so little. Especially compared to the women at the compound, all who had appetites that rivaled each of the men. Still, Louise needed adequate fuel to keep functioning on the physical level she needed every day with her career. She wasn't super slim but was larger and taller than several of the women he knew from the compound. Her size had to be an advantage when dealing with large animals. "How was your morning?"

She gave him a droll look. "I woke up to Ice yelling instructions over the top of some big filters and fans."

He grinned. "Not exactly the most peaceful of awakenings."

She shook her head. "But I certainly appreciated it. It made a huge difference in the smell of the air, and, once the policemen and the sheriff's deputies left the parking lot, it was business as usual here. There has been lots of questions about what's going on outside, but nobody seems to be too bothered about it as long as it's not happening here."

He nodded. "That will be the way of it. Once it hits the news, there might be more questions but just don't make a big deal out of it and keep moving forward."

She nodded. "That's the plan. I have a full schedule all afternoon, and then, at three, I have to head out to a couple house calls."

He winced. "Well, tag one of us at the time because you're not leaving here alone."

She nodded. "Don't worry. I have no plans to be a lone ranger here. I'm just trying to take care of my own business and look after the animals."

He nodded and finished his last few bites. "I have to give Logan a hand." He tilted his head at the leftovers and said, "Keep them close. You will need them in a little bit."

"I've eaten a ton already," she protested.

"Maybe but, when you've had very little sleep, you'll find you need more carbs to keep going."

They cleaned up the mess, and he walked to the door. "Remember, no leaving this place without somebody with you."

She nodded. "Heard and understood."

He gave her a bright smile and walked out to find Logan waiting for him. The smirk on Logan's face had Rory's back up. "What?"

Logan shrugged. "Nothing. Nothing at all."

But obviously there was something. He glanced back to see Louise taking the side door out of her office. "Whatever. Let's get at it."

"Absolutely."

He spent the next several hours testing out the security system with Logan. Stone was running the command center at home. By the time four o'clock rolled around, Rory thought he had the place in pretty decent shape. Louise was supposed to leave at three for her house calls. He turned to look and saw her vehicle was gone.

Of course it was; he'd driven her in. Yet he hadn't seen her in a couple hours. Was she still here? Suspicion set in. "Is she here?"

Logan turned from wires giving him trouble and said, "Who are you talking about?"

"Louise? I'm afraid she's taken off."

"Why would she do that?" Logan frowned, his gaze scanning the area.

"House calls," he said with a clipped tone. "She was supposed to wait for me."

"Do you know that she's left? Maybe she's still here. I didn't see her leave."

"She's gone. I can feel it."

"I don't know anything about it. Maybe she went alone." Logan grinned. "And did you consider what it means to *feel* she's gone?"

Rory slowly straightened, as if understanding the words. Then he gave a hard shake of his head, not wanting to go there. "She better not have left. I told her not to, and she agreed not to," he said. "But …" He pulled out his phone and called her. When she didn't answer, he frowned and found Nancy still manning the front desk. "Have you seen Louise?"

Nancy looked up and smiled. "Yes. She had to go out on an urgent house call."

"Do you know where she was going?"

With a couple of clicks Nancy looked up the address, wrote it down on a piece of paper and handed it to him.

"Did she go alone?" he asked, dread forming a ball in his stomach.

"I would imagine so. She always does." Nancy stared at him. "Why wouldn't she?"

He shook his head and smiled. "We were talking about going together."

Her face cleared. "The rancher showed up, saying they needed her early, asking if she could come now. Just one patient was left for her to see, so I shuffled that one over to the other doctor, and she ran out."

"Did she leave the front way?" He hadn't seen her drive away, but he'd also been busy inside. Had she gone on her own or with the rancher?

"I think so."

As he walked back outside, he stopped by Logan and said, "I drove last night. She didn't have her truck here. According to Nancy, Louise left to go to this address."

Logan slowly straightened and said, "Then she must have gone with somebody from our group."

Rory already had his phone out, calling Ice. She didn't answer, but Levi did.

"What's up?"

"Any idea where Louise is?"

There was silence on the other end. "I thought that was your job. Are you telling me that you've lost her?"

"She was supposed to let me know when she was leaving for a house call to one of the local ranchers. But she didn't. I noticed she wasn't around and talked to Nancy. She said Louise left after the owner of a ranch said she was needed early. The thing is, I drove her here last night. Did one of you bring her vehicle in? If not, I need to find out how she left. With a client or on her own?"

Levi paused and then said, "Are you thinking she was taken?"

"Well, I admit there's been easily twenty or thirty people here today. I have been working inside, but so has she. I thought she was here for sure. I expected her to call me or to find me and to let me know she had to leave because we were going together. I'll check in with the receptionist again but didn't want to raise any alarms so called you first."

"Well then, that should be your answer. She either left on her own, which I doubt since she didn't have her own wheels, or she left with somebody she trusted or she left under duress. Did you get a security feed up yet? Any sign of something happening around the parking lot? Start there. I will get Stone on the satellite."

Levi hung up, leaving Rory staring at Logan. "It's not one of us," he said tersely. "I'll talk to Nancy further and see who might have been here." He raced inside to find Nancy.

"Oh, I gave her my car. She told me about the break-in and being dropped off. She wasn't expecting to be long." She glanced at her watch and said, "She has another forty-five minutes, and then I was planning on leaving. I'm here till five normally, but I didn't get much lunch so I was hoping to leave a quarter to five."

Inside something settled. He realized he didn't need to panic. Maybe she was fine. He sent Levi a quick text. When he was done, he said, "I'll run there to make sure she's okay. To make sure we get your car back in time." Smiling away, he turned and walked out, updating Logan.

Yet inside, he wanted answers from Louise, and he wanted them now.

Chapter 10

B Y THE TIME Louise had checked out the mother and
son goats, her back was killing her, and her boots were
covered in crap, and she was so tired it was all she could do
to make her way to the car. She also knew she would have to
face Rory for leaving without him. She smiled at John. "I'm
glad you got me today. That wasn't exactly on my schedule,
but this guy needed to be seen."

In fact, he had a huge cyst she'd opened and drained. It
was pressing against his bladder, so he was leaking everywhere. More than that, he was in terrible pain. She looked
over at his mother who'd prolapsed after giving birth but was
doing better now.

"Keep an eye on the two of them. I'll give you the antibiotics for the mom, so she should be good for the night.
With any luck, this little guy's cyst will keep draining
overnight. I'll come back in the morning and take a look."

John smiled the big old weather-beaten smile she loved
so much. He'd been a client since she had first opened her
doors. She knew most of the animals here by name. John was
alone except for his animals, and she appreciated that. They
were his family, and she couldn't give them anything but the
best of care.

She walked to the pump, filled a bucket of water and
carefully washed her hands. John thanked her profusely as

they walked to her vehicle. She hopped into Nancy's car and, with a little toot, turned the small bright-red car back toward her clinic. She checked her phone and realized she had missed calls and texts. She had a rule about not interfering with her work by answering phone calls. Usually, when she was out on a farm, she had animals big and small to look after, and it was dangerous to take her attention off her work. She also knew she was only ten minutes away. By the time she called or texted in answer to all the calls, she'd already be back there. She would have to face the music anyway, and she'd rather do it all at once.

Whether Rory liked it or not, she'd literally gotten up and run after John—completely forgetting she wasn't to go alone. When she pulled the car into the clinic's parking lot, she was happy to see she was just inside Nancy's four forty-five deadline. When she hopped out, Rory and Logan stood there, both of them with their hands on their hips, glaring at her. She gave them a sweet smile, grabbed her purse, walked in and handed the keys over to Nancy. "You can leave now. Thanks for letting me use your car."

Nancy's face brightened. She hopped up from her chair, grabbed her purse and said, "Thank you so much."

Louise laughed. "No, it's me who should be thanking you. The goats were in a tough spot."

Nancy nodded. "John's a sweetheart. When he walked into the clinic, I knew for sure you would be racing out to help."

Louise walked outside with Nancy and waved her off. Then she turned to face both men, feeling the fatigue pull at her. "If you're both going to yell at me, why don't you just get it over with, and then you can tell everybody else you did, so I don't have to listen to it more than once."

At that Logan gave a half shout of laughter and turned away. "Not me," he said. "Rory roared enough for both of us."

She switched her gaze to Rory and realized he was steaming mad. As in his shoulders rumbled and shook with it. Even under the brim of his hat she could see his steely glare. She stared at his clenched fists and wondered why even the sight of him in this condition didn't send her running in fear. She knew he was seriously in control. She wondered if he ever lost it. Even if he did, she was pretty sure there would be a hole in the nearest wall and his fist would never come near her face.

She walked up to him, wondering how to disarm his temper. She dropped her purse, threw her arms around his neck and gave him a great big hug. His arms came around her and held her close. She caught the look on Logan's face as he turned to see the two of them. She winked at him. His face split into a big grin, and he turned the corner of the clinic.

"I'm so sorry. I didn't mean to worry you," she whispered against Rory's ear. "I should have sent you a text when I arrived, and, yes, I should have told you where I was going before I ever left."

His only response was to hold her closer.

She stood like that for a long moment, letting him unwind. The trouble was, she just wanted to snuggle in, close her eyes and rest. "I know you're still upset with me. But, if we can go home now, I'd really like to get some food and go to sleep." She waited for him to respond, and, when it came, it wasn't what she expected. But it made her feel so damn good.

He sighed. It seemed to roll up from his belly, through

his chest and release as a huge letting go.

She realized just how tensely he'd been holding himself and just how worried he'd been.

He took a step back, grabbed her face gently between his hands and said, "If you ever do that to me again …" and left his words hanging.

She smiled, understanding his concern came, not because she had disobeyed him or because she had been foolish, but because he had been seriously worried about her. That made her feel all that much better—and all that much worse.

"I'm so sorry," she whispered. "When John came in, needing his goats looked after, he was almost in tears. I actually have one more house call I'm supposed to make, so I have to go there now. Can you come with me, or do you need to stay here and help Logan?"

"Harrison's arrived with the parts we needed from town," Rory said. "So I'm coming with you. But I have to tell them where we're going." He grabbed her hand in his and said, "I'm not letting you go while I do it." He kept her hand in his while he talked to the other two men. They both managed to keep their faces straight, but she could see the merriment in their eyes at his behavior.

She smiled at Harrison and asked, "Will we see you tomorrow, or will you be done today?"

"I'm here to help as long as needed."

"I'll be here for sure tomorrow," Logan said. "We're hoping to get the system up and running tonight. We added a few extra elements to it. That complicated things. Plus, of course, today wasn't the easiest."

Logan looked over at Harrison and said, "We'll have to do some tests in the morning. Plus I want to see what happens on the video—see if we got the angles correct. So

I'll be back in the morning for sure."

She reached out a hand to shake Harrison's hand, and he just snorted, spreading out his arms. She walked into them for a hug. "I hadn't realized so many of Levi's men were huggers," she exclaimed.

"We weren't," Logan said. "But we've all been converted by the women in our lives."

She beamed at the two men and said, "Good, I'm glad to hear that." She turned back to Rory. "You ready to go?"

He stood in front of her, frowning. "Where are we going and how long will we be?"

She smiled. "It's about twenty minutes from here. We're going to Haggerty's Ranch. They've got two mares I need to check on." She turned toward Logan and Harrison. "We should be about forty minutes. I'll get Rory to check in when we're leaving."

Both men nodded. "You need to check in every time you do something. If you go straight home from there, let us know when you get back to the apartment. If we don't hear from you, we'll assume you're in trouble," Logan warned. "We're on high alert at all times now. Just because they've caught these two gunmen doesn't mean jack shit. Until this is over, … you have to stay safe."

She sobered. "I know. I'm sorry for taking off and not letting you guys know before." She added, "I'm sure Rory will keep a good eye on me for the rest of the evening."

The men's smirks flashed briefly and disappeared. "I'm sure he will," Harrison said in a quiet tone. "That's because he cares. We all do. Nobody wants to see you hurt when it's avoidable."

Sober and chastised, she nodded and walked toward the parking lot with Rory. "Are you okay to drive? Otherwise we can swing past my place and pick up my truck."

He shook his head. "I'll drive."

"Okay. We're taking a right as soon as we get out of the parking lot onto the main road."

They got in, buckled up, and he turned on the engine.

As he backed out, she couldn't help glancing around to make sure nobody watched them. "I wonder if I'll ever drive this section and not think of the men who died here."

"I hope not. Because it will always be a reminder to be careful and of how simple things in life can turn nasty. No, I don't want you to remember the pain and the panic and the fear. But, as a reminder of life's tough lessons, it's not a bad one."

"Any update on the two deputies?"

He nodded. "One didn't make it."

She gasped and subsided into silence. That wasn't what she'd wanted to hear. After a moment, she asked, "What about the two shooters taken into custody?"

"Like the other two, they aren't talking."

She shook her head. "I don't understand that."

"Because they know, if they do talk, they're in trouble."

"But if they don't talk, they're in trouble anyway. Plus how do their big bosses not know that these guys are spilling their guts? So what difference does it make?" she asked. "At least this way they might have a chance at getting free and clear of all this."

"But they don't know what that means. This is probably a lifestyle for them. They don't know what it's like *not* to be on the wrong side of the law and to have a normal nine-to-five job and a family to come home to. They don't think it's bad at all to be in jail. To them it's just a way of life. It's them against us."

"Until it's them against them," she retorted.

He nodded. "They know that too, but they also understand, if they break from their usual system, they'll get taken out. This way, at least being higher up the food chain than the men they killed means they might be saved."

"Meaning, it depends on how much value they have to the drug bosses?"

"Exactly."

The next few minutes were busy as she gave directions. She hoped they wouldn't be long at Haggerty's, but it was hard to say. It all depended on the mares. One had a terrible time conceiving, but she was racing stock with the purest pedigree. Haggerty desperately wanted a foal from her. Unfortunately it didn't matter how good the pedigree was if the mare couldn't breed successfully. Of course her eggs could be taken and frozen. That was certainly a possibility.

But not an option they would have to take if Mother Nature could be coaxed into cooperating. Which she must have as they'd been lucky when the mare had caught, and Haggerty had been babying her ever since.

When Louise and Rory finally pulled into the long driveway, she was happy to see Haggerty himself at the barn waiting for her.

He beamed at her. "Mona Lisa is looking lovely," he cried out.

She smiled at his pet name for the horse who had too many names to actually say them every time. Louise walked over to the mare heavy with her pregnancy. The mare nuzzled her hands and neck. Louise spent several moments talking to her and then checked her over.

"She's holding nicely, and her size is good. Her heartbeat is strong, and her vitals are steady." Then she checked the mare's cervix. "She's doing fine." Louise turned back to Haggerty. "I don't think she'll foal tonight. But I'd say, in the next four or five days, we'll be dealing with a little one."

Haggerty beamed. "I can't wait."

"What about Moonrise?"

He nodded and said, "I've got her in the stall next to us. I think she'll be first."

Moonrise was an easier case. She was just young. A little bit too young to be in this situation, but, because of her size, Louise hoped it wouldn't be a problem. They walked over to see a dusky-gray mare lying on her side in the barn. Louise talked to Moonrise, who knew her well, while gently checking her over.

"Right." She stood and faced Haggerty. "I'd say give it twenty-four, maybe forty-eight hours."

"That's what I figured." He looked to be a happy man, rubbing his hands together intently as he thought about the coming day. "It would be nice if we get through this with two live foals," he said.

He turned to Rory and shook his hand. "I don't know if she's told you anything about my babies here, but we've been trying for a couple years to get Mona Lisa to catch."

"Louise didn't have a chance to tell me too much. But I was raised in a ranching family, so I understand."

Haggerty nodded. "Nothing's quite like it."

The two men talked while Louise washed up, collected her bag and walked to Rory's vehicle. "Give me a shout if you are concerned at all when Moonrise goes into labor."

"I'm hoping she'll be okay. But you can bet, Doc, I'll be giving you a call."

After a wave goodbye, Rory backed out the vehicle, and they headed down the long driveway. "That looks like very rewarding work," he commented.

"It is when Mother Nature is good. But when she shows her bitchy side, it can get very difficult," she said quietly. "I'm not sure how Mona Lisa is going to do."

"That's tough."

She nodded. "He's had her for a long time. Raised her from a filly. Every time she miscarried, he cried a little bit more."

Once they hit the main road, she sank back into her seat and said, "I'm proud of the fact I survived all of today on that little bit of sleep. But I really could use a good night's sleep tonight."

"If we're lucky, we will get it," he said with a smile. He looked out at the highway and said, "Are you okay to go home now?"

She nodded. "Yes, I want a hot shower and to go to bed."

"What about dinner?"

"If we'd thought of it, we could have grabbed the leftover Chinese food."

"I did think of it," he said with a laugh. "It's in the back."

She twisted around, and, sure enough, the cartons sat on the back seat. "In that case, that's dinner."

"A little on the skimpy side," he warned.

"That's okay. Maybe I'll have a hot piece of toast too. Can't be bothered to do much more than that," she said, covering her mouth as a yawn threatened to overtake her.

"Home it is then."

She rested in the vehicle, trying not to even think about the crazy day she'd had. As they pulled up to her apartment, she smiled and said, "Nothing like being home." She hopped out, and, with him at her side, they worked their way up to the apartment.

When she got to the door, she pulled out her key, but he took it from her, went to push it in, only the door slipped open. He slammed the door closed and pushed her behind him.

She stared at him in horror, the color draining from her face. "What's the matter?"

"Did you lock it this morning?" he asked.

She frowned. "I don't know. I presume so. I always lock it." But she stared down at the key in his hand and wondered. Had she? If she had, then why had the door just pushed open? She took a deep heavy breath. "Can I go in?"

He shook his head. "Not alone. I don't know if somebody is in there waiting, but we're not taking the chance. Keeping you safe is my first priority." He quickly rushed her back down the stairs and out to his truck. "We'll see if the guys are still at the clinic."

She glanced at her watch and said, "If we don't contact them in five minutes, they'll be here anyway. At least they will be if they mean what they say."

He shot her a look. "Always count on them meaning what they say." He pulled out his phone and called Logan. "Are you guys at the clinic?"

"Yeah, just finished. Loaded up the truck with the rest of the tools. Why?"

"I want you to come here. Her apartment was unlocked. I have her with me back outside. Her place needs to be searched."

"Hey," she said from beside him, "I could have just stayed in the hall."

But, in the background, he could hear Logan saying,

"No problem. We'll be there in ten."

Rory turned to face her and said, "What if somebody is in the apartment? Or more than one person? What if I walked in, and they pulled a gun on me. It would be a piece of cake to grab you and drag you inside too."

She frowned at him. "So it's okay for you to go in and have somebody pull a gun on you?" She shook her head. "Hell, no. So far, the only assholes we've seen have been trigger-happy. Nobody's pulling a gun on anybody."

He gave her a flat gaze that made her squirm.

She crossed her arms over her chest and said, "You're not the boss, so stop trying to make me cower."

At that, his eyebrows rose. "I would never do that," he protested.

She thought about it and then realized he was right. He was just making sure she understood the gravity of the situation. She sagged back in her seat. "How long do you think we have to wait?"

"Just until Logan gets here."

"How did the bad guys know where I live?"

"That's easy," he said. "Just think about it. The clinic has your name on it. They can look up your personal info in no time."

She stared at the apartment building. "If they trashed anything …"

"They might have. I couldn't see much. And I didn't want to take the time to look." He peered through the windshield. "Hopefully we can see anyone as they try to leave."

"Sure, but there's a back way to the parking lot," she said. "My vehicle is there, remember?"

He nodded. "So let's drive around and take a closer

look."

"But then somebody could come out the front," she said in a reasonable tone. "You really need to leave me alone and go check it out yourself."

"Not happening." His tone held no room for defiance.

She muttered, "You're really bullheaded."

"Yes, I am. On some things."

Just as he decided whether to turn on the engine, Logan pulled up beside him. They rolled down the windows, and Harrison asked, "Have you been inside?"

Rory shook his head. "So far nobody's come out the front, and nobody's driven out of the parking lot. The property is fenced, so it's possible someone jumped it and took off that way."

Logan said, "I will park around back. We will go in that way. You two go in the front, and we'll meet up in the apartment."

Rory nodded. He hopped out and motioned to Louise to come with him. As she got out and slammed the door, she muttered, "Oh, so now I get to go inside. You could've left me in the vehicle too, you know."

"You're not to be alone. Deal with it."

She rolled her head, easing the tension in her neck. He took her hand and gently tugged her toward him. With an arm wrapped around her shoulder, he held her close. "We'll take the elevator, and the guys can take the stairs."

She raised an eyebrow at him. "Is that fair? They've had a long day."

"Do you want to take seven flights of stairs?"

She thought about it and shook her head. "I am really tired."

"Exactly."

When they reached her floor, instead of going directly to her apartment, Rory leaned against the wall across from the elevator and waited. She leaned beside him and said, "What are we doing?"

He chuckled. "Waiting."

She sighed. "I can see that much. But what else are we doing?"

"I'm not sure," he said in a thoughtful tone. "But I think we're getting to know each other. Matter of fact, we're probably past all that initial stuff and heading right into getting to know each other very well."

"But that's almost a step away from having a relationship," she said. "So unless that's in either of our plans …"

He grinned. "I really do like your sense of humor."

She shook her head. "You just like the fact you can tell me to stay, and I generally obey."

"I like that too. But it sure didn't work today when I told you not to leave the clinic alone."

"It wouldn't work again either if I had to deal with another patient, and nobody was there to go with me."

Just then Logan and Harrison walked through the stairs' double doors. The foursome then headed down the hall quietly. Logan took the far side of the apartment door with Harrison on the other side. On the count of three they entered. Rory stood at the doorway with Louise behind him. She tried to see over his shoulder or around his body, but she could see nothing clearly. Just the hall to the kitchen. She could hear the men calling out, "Clear," as they swept through her apartment. Finally Rory pushed open the door and said, "You can come in."

She shot him a hard look. "See? You brought those guys here for nothing. There's absolutely nothing wrong. I probably just forgot to lock my door." And she brushed past him, intent on getting into the house and relaxing for the first time that day. She dropped her purse on the table, kicked off her shoes and headed into the living room. There she stopped. Tears came to her eyes as she realized her apartment had been up-ended. She stood in the entrance to the living room and shook her head slowly. "Why would they do this?" she asked.

"They were looking for the drugs."

"But didn't the police tell them they had the drugs?"

"It's also a warning." Logan stood beside her, anger in his voice.

"We see this way too often. It's a threat to say, 'We know where you live. We know where you are. And we can come anytime.'"

She turned stricken eyes in his direction. "But why? Why do they care?"

"Seven of their men have died so far, and two more are locked up in the police station. I think they're desperate. And maybe they already sold the drugs and now can't deliver them." Rory placed his hands on her shoulders. "You don't need to stay here tonight," he said gently.

She twisted to look up at him. "Really? And where do you suggest I go? They'll still find me no matter which hotel I choose."

"But there's one place you can go where not only would you be safe but everybody would be more than happy to see them come and visit you."

She frowned, not understanding, until she glanced at the other men and their wide grins.

Rory said, "Come to the compound. You'll be safe there."

RORY WATCHED THE conflicting emotions wash over her face. He'd already taken a good hard look at the apartment. It was certainly cleanable. This had been done more as a threat than to cause any permanent damage. If all four of them knuckled down, they could get it cleaned up quickly. Just the guys could do it pretty fast as Louise seemed a bit in shock still. Yet he'd rather have her back at the compound where she'd be safe.

He also knew he'd been pushing her comfort button since he first met her. She wasn't ready to hide behind somebody else, and that just pissed him off more because the people at the compound were fully capable of looking after her. He didn't want to do anything that would put her in harm's way. He motioned to the living room and said, "If you're serious about staying, then it probably wouldn't take us an hour to straighten things up."

He watched as she shoved her hands in her pockets and her shoulders hunched. Body language was so indicative of moods. In a softer voice, he said, "But that doesn't mean you have to face this tonight. You're already tired, and you've been through a lot today. Come back to the compound with us. There's lots of space. Spend the night, and then tomorrow go to the clinic. We can come here afterward and straighten up. It looks to me like they did this more as a threat than anything."

Logan nodded. "I'd agree with that. There's no real damage. The couch has been flipped upside down, but it's not broken. The seat cushions were tossed, but they haven't been cut open. Nothing's been spray-painted or burned. It's just in disarray. A message."

She frowned as she leaned against the wall, staring at the

mess. Rory stepped forward and, with Logan's help, uprighted the couch. Seconds later they had the cushions back on and rearranged and tidied up the living room. Rory knew it didn't change the fact that the intruders had come once, and they would possibly come back. At least seeing her living room back to normal would reduce some of her initial shock. And that was all this was. If the intruders had been seriously looking for something, they would have done a much more thorough job.

Once they had the living room tidied up, she still hadn't said a word. Rory motioned toward the bedroom. Again it was the same thing. The bedding had been pulled off, and the mattress sent askew. The chair was upside down, and her clothes were thrown out of the closet. It wouldn't take long to put it back to rights.

"We can rehang everything in a few minutes. It won't be back exactly the way you had them, but they'll be off the floor," Rory said, standing in front of the big double closet. He loved the fact she didn't completely overwhelm the closet with her clothes. There was lots of space, particularly since no men's clothing hung there. That made him feel good. "It's certainly livable if you want to stay for the night."

"Which would put you out the least?"

He turned to look at her. "Well, I'm staying with you regardless. If you want to stay here, we can stay here. It's also easy to look after you at the compound."

Her toes tapped the floor. "Meaning?"

"Meaning, if we stay here, somebody will be at the compound to answer my phone calls, waiting to see if we have any more problems."

Logan picked up the conversation. "And we'll likely set somebody outside on watch."

"And if I'm not here? Isn't it foolish to keep up the same surveillance?"

"Unless they see you leave."

"Do we want them to see me leave?"

Rory gave her a slow smile, liking the way her mind worked. She had an agile intelligence.

"Why not set a trap? Is that feasible? I don't understand much about all this stuff, but it would seem to me that, if they're watching this place, then it's me they're after. So we should let them either have me or think they're getting me and make sure we take them out instead."

Logan gave a low whistle. "I like the way your mind works, Louise."

She shrugged but pink stained her cheeks. "I want this over," she said firmly. "The only way seems to be for us to come face-to-face with them and make them realize I don't have the drugs anymore." She pinched the bridge of her nose. "And the people at the top need to get the message, not those at the bottom."

"Doesn't mean we will catch the ones above that though," Rory reminded her. "This is a decent-size organization."

She nodded, took a deep breath and said, "I know you won't like this, but ..."

"Then don't say it," he snapped, already pissed because he knew what she was going to say. "No way are you going to be bait." He crossed his arms over his chest and glared at her.

She crossed her arms over her chest and glared at him, almost in a mocking imitation. But the look on her face said she wasn't trying to insult him. She was showing as much defiance and determination as he was.

Inside he was smiling. She really was cute.

"This can't go on. So many people have been hurt already. I can't let my staff or my animals get hurt." She let her gaze roam from one man to the other.

Rory watched as she tried to give them all a bright smile.

Only it faltered when she added, "I trust you guys. I need you to let them catch me, and then you come after me and save me."

"What makes you think they have any interest in capturing you?" Logan asked.

It's a good thing he was talking because Rory was too furious to let any words out. That she thought he'd let her get caught by these assholes was beyond belief.

She pivoted her gaze to Logan. "What do you mean?"

His voice dropped to a very gentle whisper. "You do remember that, at the first opportunity, they shot everybody they could, regardless of who was there or what they may have had to say."

Her skin paled. She nodded. "But they want something from me."

"They might. Or they will give you two seconds to answer before they shoot you dead." Harrison walked over and said, "You need to rethink that plan. I get what you're trying to do. But there has to be another way."

"So what is it then?" she challenged him. "As soon as you guys come up with an answer that makes sense, I'm all for it. But, right now, nothing makes sense. If I leave here, they will follow me. That means everyone at the compound is in danger. That won't make anyone happy."

"It will make *all* of us happy," Rory snapped. "There we're fully prepared for an attack. Here you're just a sitting duck."

"What happens if they try to take me out on the way to the compound?"

"That's a possibility." He nodded. "Considering they shot the deputies and the other two men while they were driving. There's no guarantee in any of this. But, if they know you're here, they *will* come back."

"Let them assume I'm here. Set up a trap, and catch them when they arrive."

The men stared at her and then exchanged glances.

Rory said, "Or what if we don't smuggle you out because they might realize what we're doing. What if you stayed in another apartment in the building?"

"How will we do that?"

"We ask the manager if there's an empty apartment and rent it," he suggested. "And, no, I don't know that it's a possibility, but, if we do smuggle you out, we are taking the chance of getting caught in transit."

"Or let's just stay here, and you guys can protect me." She gave him a very sweet smile.

"Oh, no, you don't," he said. "No using feminine wiles on me."

She batted her lashes at him and laughed. "Why? Won't they work?"

He shot her a look and turned his attention to the space around him. "It's possible they are watching your place. Would having us here now be a change in pattern?"

"Yes, it would be," she admitted. "I don't currently have a partner. I'm not dating too often, and I work too much. So any activity at all is already going to be a change in my pattern."

He nodded thoughtfully and glanced at Logan. "They wouldn't have been watching her apartment before the delivery so not sure how much of an issue it is now."

"Even a small issue is too much. I say she goes back to the compound." Logan looked around and said, "Two of us can stay here just in case. Leave her vehicle here."

She shook her head. "I could get shot on the way."

"You could get shot anywhere," Rory said, rubbing his temple. Just then his phone rang. He glanced down to see who it was. "Ice, we're at her apartment."

"What does it look like?" Ice asked.

"Trashed. Not completely as in the cushions aren't cut open, and the TV isn't broken. Just everything tossed in disarray."

"Bring her here."

"I suggested that, but she's fighting it."

"Why?"

"She wants to set a trap with herself as bait." He glared at Louise while he walked around the living room, distancing himself from her so he could talk privately. "I told her that wasn't happening."

"But it is a good idea," Ice said. "Just not necessarily with her being the bait."

"You mean, put in a bogey? Set a trap but have somebody else take her place? Do we have anybody who can do that?"

"I am the same build, just my hair's the wrong color. But, if I wore a wig, that's a possibility."

"She won't like that idea."

"Of course she won't. Neither will Levi," Ice said in a wry tone. "But, if we have plenty of security around, we'll be fine. Bring her home. We'll discuss it and set up a plan." And Ice hung up.

"Forget it," Louise said. "I'm not going."

"She wants to talk to you. She likes your idea about setting a trap. But she wants you back at the compound where we can devise a plan. We have lots of men available. She wants to make sure we've got all the bases covered."

He deliberately didn't mention the use of somebody else in her place because he knew she would argue against it. She tapped her fingers on her arms, and he added, "Alfred's already got a place set for you at the table," he lied. But he also knew perfectly well Alfred would easily add a plate without a qualm.

She sighed. "Okay, but I want to come back, and I want to be heavily involved in this."

He nodded and smiled. "Let's go talk to the gang. See what we come up with."

With Harrison leading the way, she stepped out the door. As Rory followed, Logan grabbed his shoulder and said in a low voice, "Do you think she will go for it?"

He thought about it for all of a second, then shook his head. "Hell no."

Chapter 11

A S SHE PULLED into the parking lot at the compound, she admitted it felt weird. She'd always been here in a professional capacity as a vet, not as a client. She didn't like the change. Knowing she was here because it was a safety net—and spending the night—felt wrong. She was bad at asking for help, and, at this point, it felt like she was in the uncomfortable position of needing a lot of help.

It wasn't her style. She'd always been fiercely independent. At the moment her relationship with Ice and Levi was getting a tad too complicated.

As for her relationship with Rory, she didn't understand what was happening, yet obviously something was blossoming. She wasn't against it. He was a good man, and he'd certainly been a huge help.

He was also a strong alpha male, and that in itself was incredible sexy. Even better he seemed unaware of it. That there was a physical attraction was obvious, and that was good too. But it was hard to imagine any kind of a relationship at the moment with so much stress involved. At the same time it was also almost impossible to ignore how very much her heart and soul were susceptible to his particular brand of charm.

She also hated that she was connecting to Rory over this nightmare. She'd love to get to know him more, but it worried her that maybe what she felt wasn't real. Although it felt real. More real than she'd felt in a long time.

When she got out and closed the truck door, he walked around and held out his hand. "Don't be nervous," he scolded.

"You know them as equals," she said quietly, willing him to understand. "This feels different."

At her words, he stopped and studied her for a long moment. "I can understand that," he said. "But just because you're here and need help doesn't make you any less than them. Everybody has a particular skill set. Yours is with the animals. Theirs is with security."

She considered that for a long moment, then the door opened, and puppies cascaded toward them. She bent down to scoop up one particular wiggling ball of energy and buried her face in his fur. "My, look how big you're getting."

The puppy wiggled so hard trying to reach her face that she couldn't resist him and let him clean one cheek. Then she hugged him tightly again. Rory gently stroked her back, offering comfort, somehow understanding on an altogether different level what she needed. Then she handed the puppy to him and said, "Your turn."

She reached down to snag another one and saw Alfred at the door with a puppy in his arms. "I guess it wasn't a bad deal to bring them?" she asked.

Alfred smiled and shook his head. "No, we've all fallen in love with them."

"Anna was afraid of that."

Alfred beamed. "You mean, Anna was smart enough to *know* that," he corrected.

Louise chuckled softly at first and then in great rolling waves of laughter as she realized just how sneaky Anna had been. Because, between the men who had their separate living places here and the others who lived within the actual compound, there was a good chance not one of these puppies would end up adopted anywhere else but here. The doors beside her opened, and Ice stepped through.

She took one look at Louise, her arms full of puppy, and grinned. "I don't know how you can possibly not keep every animal that comes through your clinic," Ice said with a big smile. She held out her arms, and Louise passed her the puppy.

"It's hard," Louise admitted. "It's one of the reasons I do a lot of work for Anna. Whenever I get strays, we work out a deal where she takes them until we can get them adopted out. Otherwise I'd keep them all."

Ice ushered her into the kitchen. "Alfred is ready to serve dinner."

"Thanks for the invite," Louise said a tad more formally than normal, still uncomfortable with her reason for being here.

"You're part of us. Don't be formal. Alfred's always happy to feed somebody else. Besides, we need to make some plans. We have to pull the plug on the drug crew and get the control back in our hands."

Louise liked the way Ice thought. And she was right. "You're correct. I feel like a victim. A puppet whose strings are pulled by somebody else. It's really frustrating. I want it to stop, but I don't know how to make that happen."

"That's where we come in," Levi said. He leaned back in a big chair at the table. Louise stopped and contemplated the massive table in front of her, set for what looked like several dozen people. "How many people is Alfred serving every night?"

"Well, right now, counting only those in the house, I think we've got sixteen."

Louise shook her head. Alfred walked in just then, pushing a large cart. He took one look at her standing there and motioned for her to take a seat. "Hurry up and sit down," he said. "Bailey is coming with the other trays."

She took a seat beside Rory and watched as Alfred emptied the cart by putting heaped platters of food up and down the table. "Alfred, you're a dream to be able to cook for this many all the time."

He chuckled. "It's what I do. You do what you do. I do what I do."

How very true. These men couldn't set bones or fix tomcats, and she couldn't possibly cook a meal like this for this many people or set up security or bait a trap for some assholes making her life difficult. It really was about everybody having their own talents and contributing where they could, doing what they could do. She watched as everybody served themselves from the platters, even as Bailey came around with another cart. She had vegetables and salads and buns. When she got to Louise, she grinned and asked, "Are the puppies okay?"

"The ones I saw so far look great," Louise said with a big smile. She watched the relief and love blossom on Bailey's face. Louise realized again how absolutely right Anna had been to place them here. As Louise let her focus return to the table, she caught sight of Levi's thundering frown. But there was no heat in it.

Then he shrugged.

Her gaze twinkling, she said, "You knew that would happen."

"I love them too," he confessed. "But we're not keeping

them."

"We aren't keeping six," Ice corrected with a smirk.

Trying to head off an argument he must have heard many times over, Rory reached for the platter in front of him and dragged it slightly closer, saying, "Serve yourself, Louise, before there's nothing left."

"I can't imagine there would be nothing left. A ton of food is here."

"Really?" he asked. He motioned to the other end of the table and said, "Take another look."

Several platters were empty or almost empty. She figured the bread was to fill up some of those deep holes in the men. Dinner was roast chicken, cut in quarters. She didn't think she could handle a whole quarter, but Rory obviously did as he placed it on her plate and then held out a large Caesar salad for her to take or not as she chose. It was her favorite. She dished up the salad beside the chicken and dug in. "I'll be lucky if I eat this much."

Levi looked at her. "Are you kidding? Almost every one of the women here eat more than you."

"I've never been a big eater," she confessed. "Maybe because I've never had this kind of food before. I'd probably eat a lot more if I lived here," she admitted.

Ice nodded. "Good food is the heart of a good family."

Louise realized just how much she liked Ice—her philosophy, her mannerisms, her gentle soul and steely personality. Not many people would fool her. But she would give the shirt off her back if she thought it would make somebody else's life easier.

Dinner was a quiet affair as everybody ate. Obviously thoughts were heavy as nobody brought up much lighthearted conversation. When she was done, Louise pushed back her plate with a happy sigh. Alfred was down at the far end. She leaned forward slightly and said, "Alfred, that was delicious. Thank you so very much."

He looked up with a pleased smile on his face. "You only ate the chicken and salad. You could have had some roasted vegetables."

She grinned. "I did wonder if there is dessert."

Everybody turned to look at Alfred who raised innocent eyebrows and said, "I didn't make any dessert tonight."

A shock wave went through the table as people realized they might not get a sweet treat at the end of their meal.

Louise shrugged. "That's all right. I don't get dessert most of the time."

Bailey chuckled. "What he means is, he didn't make the dessert tonight, but I did."

A cheer went up around the table.

"Dare I ask what it is?" Louise asked. "How lucky for Alfred to have found you."

Alfred nodded. "I'd be lost without Bailey as this place has grown so much, and there are just that many more vegetables to prep and roast."

"And custards to bake and muffins to mix and cakes to throw in the oven," Bailey added with a laugh. She smiled at Louise. "I got a hankering for cream puffs today."

Levi straightened. "We've got cream puffs coming?" He looked at his plate, as if measuring to see if he still had room. "In that case, … they're really light. I can get a couple down."

Louise watched as all the men inhaled a mess of food. When they were done, everyone picked up their knife and fork and plate and took them into the kitchen, a process they'd done many times over, and then they all came back again in a single line.

Rory took her plate even though she would have been happy to have taken care of her own. When he sat down beside her again, a stack of clean plates were in his hands. He took two and passed the rest down. Before she knew it, Bailey was back with more platters, … platters of cream puffs. She set three down, spanning the long table. Levi grabbed the platter closest to him and dragged it to the end where the four of them sat. Ice snagged one and put it on her plate. Louise watched as Levi took three. Rory looked at Levi's plate, nodded and grabbed three for himself. Looking at Ice's plate, Louise took one cream puff and laughed. "I can see why you grab fast around this place."

"You have to do the same with coffee. Speaking of which, there's a fresh pot."

Rory pointed to the sideboard. "Would you like a cup?"

A few minutes later, over coffee, Ice brought up the subject sitting in the back of Louise's mind. "Anyone have suggestions about Louise's issue?"

Louise was surprised that everybody in the compound was involved. A lot of the women were here too, but then it was part of the life here. If they sheltered somebody who was potentially in danger, and that danger came home, they needed to know as well. She settled back to see what people would say.

Levi said, "Louise wants to set a trap. Take back control and find a way to get the men coming after her."

"We always prefer to take control away from the bad guys," Stone said from the far end of the table. "Waiting for somebody else to act is incredibly frustrating."

"The question is whether they'll attack her apartment or they'll come here," Rory said. "We deliberately left a slow trail so anyone watching could follow. Logan and Harrison stayed back and went a different route just in case somebody was trying to follow them." He looked over at Logan with a raised eyebrow.

Logan shook his head. "No sign of anyone that I could see. Stone, do you have anything to add to that?"

"Nobody following you on your way here."

"Okay, so they didn't necessarily follow her here, but we'll assume they've tracked her to this point. Which begs the question, will these men make a move on her, or will they either rescue or take out their men currently in jail at the police station first?"

"Or both at the same time. Which would be a better idea on their part."

"If they have the manpower, yes, it would be," Rory said. "Divide and conquer."

"Meaning?" Louise asked.

"Meaning, if they attack the police station, it will keep the police focused at home, leaving the attackers open to come after you here."

She frowned. It was hard to think of things like that. She'd spent her life trying to save animals. These animals were spending a lifetime trying to kill people. They came from such different worlds. "My apartment is empty. What's the chance they'll go back there?"

"They didn't get anything the first time, so I highly doubt they'll go back. Unless they think you're there."

"In which case I should head over there myself," Ice said.

Louise turned to look at her. "Why you?"

"Because I will go as a dead ringer for you. I have the same body type but different colored hair. I have wigs for just this type of occasion."

Louise opened her mouth to protest, but Rory reached over and squeezed her fingers. "It's what we do. Remember that."

Stricken, she turned her gaze from one to the other. "What if one of you gets hurt? Because of me?"

"If anybody touches Ice, there'll be a hell of a lot more brimstone and hellfire coming their way," Levi said, his voice hard, his hand covering Ice's.

Louise slumped in place. "Send me instead. You guys just make sure you're ready for whoever comes after me." She studied Ice. "What if they shoot you when you get out of the vehicle?"

The two women stared at each other.

"She's got a point," Levi said. "They've proven they've got sharpshooters." He frowned, contemplating the idea.

Ice shrugged. "You know we have to take a chance on some of this."

"No, we don't," Louise said.

"We've already decided they want to talk to you, not just shoot you," Rory said. "They've had plenty of opportunities to do that already, so keep that in mind."

She winced. "Great, just what I want to think about. The only question they could possibly ask me is about the case of drugs. And we already said the cops have it."

Levi's phone went off. He pulled it out and checked the caller. "It's the police department." He pushed his chair back and walked a few paces away so he could hear the conversation better.

Louise looked at Ice and Rory. Both watched Levi. She twisted to see the look of surprise on his face. He shook his head and kept talking, but he walked farther away. She sagged back in her chair. "It's not good news, is it?"

Rory grabbed her hand and held it firmly in his. "It doesn't matter what kind of news it is. You're here, and you're safe."

She gave a shuddering breath and smiled at him. "Thank you for that."

A lopsided grin slipped out, and he said, "You're welcome."

RORY CAUGHT ICE'S gaze. Had she figured out the phone call? He'd assumed there'd been an attack on the police station. The question was, how many more were dead? This gang was cleaning up pretty fast. Whether that would be enough or whether they still felt they had to come back after Louise, he didn't know. Levi continued his phone conversation. When he put away the phone and walked back, he said, "Change of plans."

Everybody at the table turned to look at him.

"One of the men being held at the police station is dead."

Rory glanced to see the color bleaching out of Louise's face. "One of the shooters?"

Levi nodded. "None of the cops were hurt. The shooter ingested poison somehow. A full investigation is underway. Now they have to look at their own men. They had a cleaning crew in today they haven't been able to locate, or maybe the man being held had something hidden on his person he could take himself."

"He would know what was coming. Maybe he had an opportunity to take himself out first."

"The good news is, the second man is talking. Once he realized his companion was dead, he agreed to cooperate with the authorities."

"Has he offered anything useful yet?" Rory asked.

"He's in the interrogation room right now. I trust Detective Mannford to figure this out."

"Excellent," Ice said. "Should I call him?"

Levi nodded. "He has the files in front of him. He's going through those before speaking to the gunman but would like to connect with you."

She poured a fresh cup of coffee and said, "I'll call him now then." And she walked out.

"Is this detective somebody you've worked with before?" asked Louise.

"Several times." Levi sat down again and said, "For the moment we won't try to bait a trap. We'll see what information they can get from this other man, while our goal here remains to keep you safe. So, whether you like it or not, you're here for the night. We will get you to work in the morning, and somebody will be at the clinic all day with you. It's Saturday tomorrow, so I presume it's a full day?"

She nodded. "Yes, it is. No surgeries but my schedule is fully booked."

"Then there's Haggerty's mare. Do you think you'll see Moonrise?"

Louise turned to Rory and smiled. "Only if Moonrise is in trouble. It's Mona Lisa I'm more concerned about."

At the confused looks, Rory explained the mares were both heavy with foals.

The news lit up everyone's faces.

Alfred walked toward Louise with a stack of towels. "I have a room set up for you. It's on the third floor. Rory can show you where it is. I just took these out of the laundry. You can have a nice hot shower or a bath if you want. I'm sure the guys will entertain you tonight. There are lots of movies and other activities. I'll take the puppies outside for a walk, and then I'll retire to my quarters." He gave a wave and headed back to the kitchen.

"How long has he been here with you?"

"Since we first formed the company," Levi admitted. "I'd be lost without him."

She glanced at the stack of towels and then turned to Rory. "We should've grabbed clothes and an overnight bag. Why didn't I do that?"

"I think we were a little too busy dealing with the shock of having your place turned upside down."

"Still it was foolish. I have to go to the clinic tomorrow in the same clothes I wore today. And that's after working on several horses today."

"We can run past your place first thing in the morning on our way to the clinic. You can do a quick change, and then we can carry on."

She brightened. "Thank you. That'd be great."

Rory stood and said, "Levi, if there's nothing else to discuss right now, let me get Louise settled in her room, and I'll return."

Levi glanced at him. "Don't bother coming back. Head to the office. Once Ice is off the phone, we'll have a meeting." He glanced at the other men at the table. "Give us twenty and then come up."

The men nodded.

Rory snagged his hat off the sideboard, then reached out a hand to Louise.

She stood. With a smile to everyone, she let Rory lead her down the hall. Rory watched the amazement build on her face as she took in her surroundings. "It's an amazing place."

"It's all stone and concrete," he said. "It's a damn fortress." He led her to the elevator and pushed the button.

"An elevator? Is this a house or an office building?"

"It's almost an apartment building at this point." Rory nudged her in as the double doors opened. When they arrived on the third floor, he led her to the appointed room.

She stared in both directions. "How many bedrooms are up here?"

"At least a dozen, I think, although some aren't necessarily being used as bedrooms right now. The offices are on this floor too."

He walked to his room, opened the door and put his hat on his dresser, turning to give her a moment to see inside. "This is my room. Alfred always puts our guests next to the person who brought them." He moved to the next door and smiled. "This is for you."

She stepped inside and realized the bedding had already been turned back for her. The window was open, and the curtain flowed gently in the breeze.

"This is beautiful." She smiled. "This place is absolutely amazing."

"It is. Not all the bedrooms have en suites, but most of them do." He motioned toward the door on the far side. "There's your bathroom. Do you want to have a shower now, maybe get cleaned up a bit?"

"I still have to put dirty clothes back on though, so I'd rather shower before bed."

"Not quite, Ice is grabbing you a change of clothes. You're both about the same size."

As he finished speaking Ice walked in with a stack of clothing in her arms. "These should do, at least temporarily.

You've got time for a quick wash and change but that's it."

Surprised and touched, Louise accepted the clothes, turning to stare at Rory as Ice left.

"Then in that case, do what you need to do." He checked his watch, adding, "We're a few minutes ahead of our meeting."

"Back quick," she walked to the bathroom, overjoyed at being able to get into clean clothes. But not wanting to take too much time, and a pro at cleaning up after working with animals, she washed fast. When she was done, she dressed quickly amazed at how well Ice's clothes fit her own lean body. Her skin now shiny pink, she opened the bathroom door to find Rory leaning against the door, on his phone.

She walked to the window as she braided her hair. "This place is huge."

"It is. And they're expanding all the time."

She nodded. "I see the heavy equipment down below. What's that for?"

He stood beside her, his hand resting on her shoulder. "They're putting in a big pool, hot tub and tennis court area. Fitness is very important to everybody here."

"Hmm, wow," she said in awe. "This is unbelievable."

"I think that's how we all feel. Every one of us is damn glad to be here."

She turned to smile at him. "You don't miss the ranch?"

"It took me a long time to leave. I should have handed the ranch back over to my brother earlier. It was hard, but it wasn't my place. Even though it's where I grew up, it was my dad's and my brother's. It wasn't my life. But it took me days to deal with the grief of leaving that lifestyle. Something about working the raw land sat perfectly in my soul. But I also realized I wasn't ready to step out of life to that extent either. I still wanted to do a lot more. I needed to do a lot more. Levi offered me the perfect opportunity to do that. Down the road, who knows?"

He smiled and with his arm tucked around her shoulder led her back to the door. "You okay to go to the meeting?"

Her footsteps slowed. "I am, but I can't say it's where I really want to be."

He frowned and looked down at her. "Where do you want to be?"

She slipped her arms around his waist and rested her head against his chest. "Right here."

Chapter 12

LOUISE WASN'T EXACTLY sure what had brought her to make that move. Maybe it was just a need to be held and to know everything would be okay. Which was kind of foolish considering she was here in this massive place with more security than she had ever seen. But when his arms wrapped around her, and he held her close, she realized that was really what she was looking for—the comfort of human touch in times of stress. Yet she didn't want that with just anyone—only with him. She squeezed him gently and then stepped back. "Just needed a hug. Thank you."

He focused on her, a serious look in his eyes. "Everybody needs hugs now and again. And you should never have to ask."

"I didn't really ask," she said cheekily.

He grinned. "Well, maybe I'm asking." He opened his arms.

She stepped back into them, once more laying her head against his chest. For a long moment they just stood like that. Offering, accepting and taking as needed. An odd buzzing noise sounded through the room. She tilted her head back and said, "What's that?"

"That's Levi calling for the meeting."

She nodded. "Then we better go and attend. Considering this is all about me."

He led the way to the office on the same floor. For some reason she had figured it would be some other third floor. It seemed odd to have bedrooms and offices together. As she stepped inside a large room, she could see another dozen people there. Most she knew. She smiled at everyone and took a seat closest to Rory.

Ice stood and said, "I've just spoken with Detective Mannford. The second shooter is talking. He's handed over names, dates, his bank account to track payments. He also supplied the names of their eight people killed, including the poisoned shooter. This surviving gunman's accepting responsibility, along with his dead partner, for all five shooting deaths. They were under direct orders to make sure nobody was left to talk."

"Who are *they?*" Rory asked. "Exactly what are we up against?"

Ice smiled. "It's not a new drug cartel. It's a new arm of an old drug cartel. They've been operating in the US for a long time. Based out of Colombia. They're trying to get a new product across the border. What we ended up doing was messing up their distribution network."

"And how did that happen exactly?" Louise asked. "I didn't do anything."

"They were operating within successful businesses well-known for international deliveries, using those easily recognized delivery trucks to disguise their drug-running, while making regular deliveries. This route had a new driver. He handed over the wrong shipment."

"Is it that simple?" Louise asked. "Really?"

Ice nodded. "That's all it took. How many times have we either lost or gotten the wrong shipment? It happens. The fact that it was a new guy is what concerns me. Sounds like the cartel is growing and is short on trained men."

"Too bad he had to die for his mistake," Louise said quietly.

"Eight dead bodies now," Ice said. "All belonging to the same crew. Detective Mannford thinks they are closing down the arm of the cartel and moving to a new location. They are just cleaning up their tracks."

"I would," Louise said. "I would move across the country and change my delivery system completely."

"That's quite possibly what they are doing. The police still don't have the analysis back on the drugs yet. The labs apparently are overrun, so they've been a little too busy."

Louise gave a half snort. "Every lab in the country is overrun. But obviously it's some drug the cartel wants."

"According to the informant, it's heroin. And it's very pure."

"So how do we stop it? Did they give any details about where their warehouse is? How are the drugs coming across the border?"

"Detective Mannford is planning a sting operation tonight," Levi said. "That's why we're waiting to set any trap with Louise or her look-alike. Let Mannford see what he can come up with overnight. If he can bring down the bulk of that arm, then we should be free and clear. But, until we know how his sting operation went, I don't want to set anything up that'll divert men from that location."

In a convoluted way Louise understood that. "So we just wait till morning?" she asked.

"And quite possibly all day tomorrow."

"Good. Anything else?"

A few other questions were asked. Ice answered those and then said, "You're on your own until I call you again."

Everybody got up and filed out. Realizing it was already past nine, Louise walked toward her bedroom. Rory was at her side. She stopped at the doorway and said, "I'm going to shower and go to bed."

He nodded. "Have a good night then."

He walked past, and she was disappointed. For some reason she thought there would be a good-night kiss, but then had they really progressed down that path? Inside she turned to close the door, only to find him standing in the doorway, his arms crossed his chest.

She glanced at him in surprise. "I thought you left already."

"I did, but I came back."

"Why? What's up?" She glanced around him. "Did Ice need something?"

He shook his head. "No, but I do."

She opened the door wider and motioned him inside. "What is it you need then?"

He pulled her into his arms and whispered, "This." He lowered his lips to hers and kissed her. It wasn't just a good-night kiss. It was a "Hey, are we in this together?" kiss. An "Am I doing this alone, or are we really feeling something between us?" kiss.

Sensing the tentativeness behind it, she wrapped her arms around his neck and held him close, kissing him with all the enthusiasm she possessed.

Responding to her, he tugged her tight against him and kissed her hard. When he finally pulled his head back, he said, "Now that's a good-night kiss."

He stepped away, and, with a grin, he walked to the door.

She raced behind him, opened the door, checked to

make sure the hall was empty and said, "How was that a good-night kiss?"

Startled, not expecting her to come after him, he stared down at her. "Are you saying it wasn't a good-night kiss?"

"Hell no. That was a prelude to a 'we're going to bed for the night' kiss," she snapped. She fisted her hands on her hips. "Just what are we doing here?"

He shook his head. "Anything you want. I'm open. Definitely interested. Free and single. You?"

She nodded. "Free and single, definitely yes. And interested, yes. So?"

He retraced his steps, a twinkle in his eyes. "So? What does that mean?"

"It means, are we working toward a relationship?" she asked in confusion. "I'm not really sure how we got to this point. And it seems very strange to have to actually question it."

"Why are you?"

"Because I feel like so much of my life right now is out of control that I want to have some control over this."

Understanding lit his gaze. "Okay, you're in control. What is it you want to do?"

She stared at him for a long moment and smiled. "I'd like to have a shower, and I'd like to go to bed. But I don't want to go alone."

The look on his face was almost comical.

She chuckled. "Or is that a little too much control?"

He shook his head slowly. "No, you haven't brought out handcuffs and a whip yet, so I'm thinking we're still on safe ground."

But instead of laughing she was interested. He on the other hand looked worried, and she felt her heart bubble with joy. "Can't say I have ever tried either of those two things. Not normally my style." She watched the relief whisper across his face and chuckled out loud. "Doesn't mean I might not be interested in trying though."

He flashed a wicked grin at her. "With you, I'm more than happy to go in any direction you want to take."

"Of course riding crops would be more my style."

Instead of backing away he took a step closer, nudging her deeper into her bedroom. He closed the door behind him with a hard *click* and said, "According to Ice, we have all night. What was that about a shower first?"

"Join me?" she asked, and then, with a laugh, she raced toward the bathroom.

RORY GAVE A shout of laughter and chased after her. The bathroom door almost closed in front of him. He hesitated and then pushed it open and stepped inside. Just as he looked around, a bra sailed toward him, followed by light-hearted female laughter from inside the large glass shower.

Water poured down, and she gasped at the coolness.

"You're supposed to wait until it warms up first," he said, chuckling.

"Well, you could come in here and warm me up instead. Unless you don't like water?" Her head peered around the corner of the shower. "It never occurred to me that maybe you prefer to shower alone."

He was already pulling off his clothes. "Good, don't stop and analyze what you think I want. Be yourself. That's all I would hope for."

She gave him a brilliant smile and said, "In that case you had better hurry up."

He kicked off his shoes, dropped his pants and stepped out of his boxers and socks all at once. He didn't need a second invitation. He joined her in the shower, his gaze going to the smooth creamy skin in front of him. She was long and lean and trim. He reached for the bar of soap and stepped toward her. Against her head he murmured, "Do you need your back washed?"

She leaned her head forward, pulling her hair to the side and said, "Absolutely."

He turned her slightly, so the water could sluice down her skin. Then he proceeded to soak and scrub her back, her buttocks and her long legs. When he came up the front of her body, his movements were slower, sexier. Long fingers stroked her flat belly, flicking over her hip bones, slipping into the curve of her waist and up to cup her plump breast. His other hand dropped to stroke the bar of soap through the creamy curls at the juncture of her legs, reaching down to kiss her breasts now at eye level. He covered the tips with his mouth and suckled lightly at first, then harder.

She moaned, swaying in his arms.

"Easy, sweetheart. Take it easy." But he wouldn't let up his torment, cupping and stroking and soothing as he nibbled and teased his way across the silky flesh in front of him. By the time he reached her chin, she was pliant in his arms, leaning partially against the shower wall, her head back, letting the water flow over them both. He straightened and stared. "You're such a mermaid."

She opened her eyes and gave him a beautiful smile. "As a little girl that's all I ever wanted to be." She slung her arms around his neck and pulled him close. "Are you willing to be my merman?"

He dropped his lips against hers and whispered, "Absolutely."

With her warm slick skin against his, a shudder rippled down his spine. His erection pressed against the juncture of her thighs, but he didn't want this moment to end. He didn't want to rush anything. He hadn't expected to be here tonight and wanted to savor every moment. They had all night according to Ice. But he also knew just how quickly plans could change. There were no guarantees. He wanted to make the most of this first time he had with her. His hands gently exploring, he took the time to caress every silky inch of her, to stroke, to tease his lips across her shoulder, up to the crease of her neck to her jawline. What he really loved was she just let him. She didn't try to caress and stroke back, she didn't participate in any way; she just soaked up every ounce of attention he willingly gave her. When he stopped, she opened her eyes and whispered, "My turn?"

He grinned. "If you would like a turn."

Her eyes gleamed in the steamy half light. "Oh, I want a turn."

Very quickly he reached for the shower wall for support.

Her hands danced and teased and tickled and stroked along his shoulders, his ribs, his chest and his hips, down his thighs, everywhere but where he was desperate to have her. Of course she knew that.

He groaned as she stroked the inside of his thighs, feeling the tension coiling inside him. "Don't do too much of that," he warned, "or this will be over before it starts."

"Oh, no, it won't be," she promised. "I plan on having all night."

"I thought the idea was to get some sleep," he teased.

"Sometimes healthy loving is as good as a four-hour shot of sleep."

"Isn't that the truth," he murmured. He'd found that himself, although it didn't always work out that way. Sometimes it was a prelude to a heavy deeper sleep. But often it was a rejuvenating shot in the arm that kept him pepped up and going for hours.

Stepping behind him, she reached around and hugged him close, her breasts flattening against his back. She just rested in that position, her head against his shoulders, holding him close.

And he smiled. "Needing that hug again?"

When she nipped his back, he groaned, so she did it again.

He groaned a second time.

"Maybe I do want that riding crop," she said with a laugh. She slipped her hands over his buttocks, gently caressing the crease between. His body jerked, his erection ready for action. She moved to face him, her hand sliding across and around into the curls at the base of his groin and then sliding up past his erection, over his belly, his ribs, up his chest to stroke his head. There she grabbed his hair and pulled him down firmly, and she kissed him in an open-mouthed tongue-warring kiss that promised so much …

He wrapped his arms around her tightly, his temperature rising and his blood pounding. Finally he couldn't stand it anymore. He tore free and said, "Here or on the bed?"

She grinned. "Here, then the bed."

His gaze widened, but he didn't hesitate. He picked her up, her back flat against the shower wall, shifted her hips so her legs were wrapped around his waist, and he plunged deep. She gasped and arched in his arms. Tension coiled deep inside as he slid in, reaching for and finding the heart of her. She wrapped her arms around his neck and started to ride. He gritted his teeth, as he tried to not end this too soon. Her taking over at this point wasn't what he expected, but it was a hell of a deal.

It was all he could do to hold her safely in place as she moved gently, slowly sliding up and down his shaft, and then faster and faster until she arched in his arms and cried out.

Instantly he pushed her gently back against the shower wall and pounded against her, driving deeper and deeper until his own climax ripped through him. He shuddered in place, his head dropping to rest against hers, the two caught in their moment of complete togetherness.

Warm water rained over them both. When he could, he reached out a hand to shut off the water.

She chuckled. "I guess we're not saving water this way, are we?"

"Nope, but it's worth every penny."

Slowly she separated from him, turned the water back on, quickly rinsed off, stepped from the shower and handed him a towel. "I'm tired, but I'm not exhausted."

"Good," he said seriously. "Because I really don't want our first night to end so fast."

She stepped into the bedroom, pulled the bedding back all the way and lay down. She had the towel under her wet hair, but she held up her arms for him. "Perfect. Even if you just hold me. It's so nice to be with you."

Touched, he tucked her close against him and wrapped one towel around her wet locks, then used his second towel to gently dry the parts of her he could reach. "You are very special, you know that?"

She shook her head. "No. If I was special I would have had a relationship these past five years."

He leaned up on a forearm and stared down at her. "Five

years?"

She nodded and gave him a wry smile. "Apparently I'm picky."

He lowered his head and gently kissed her lips. "So am I. Sounds like we're made for each other."

She reached her arms around his neck, tugged him closer and whispered, "Prove it."

He crushed her against him and showed her all over again just how perfect they were together.

Chapter 13

LOUISE AWOKE THE next morning to a heavy leg over her thighs and a heavy arm across her chest. She smiled. Even in his sleep Rory was a man who knew what he wanted. She could appreciate that. She had done plenty of taking last night too—and giving. She reached for her cell phone to check the time. It was already six in the morning. She didn't want the day to start. The night had been so special; she wanted more. But were more to come? She hoped so.

She stroked his arm and whispered against his ear, "It's time for me to get up."

But, instead of letting her go, his arm tightened, tugging her closer.

She chuckled. "It's after six."

"So?" mumbled Rory, his voice sleepy.

She patted his shoulder, slipped out from underneath his arm and leg and stood. "If nothing else, I have to go to the bathroom." She used the facilities and quickly washed up. Her hair was a tangled mess. She braided it as best she could, clipped it at the end. Today would be another long day, and she needed her hair out of the way. As she returned to the bedroom, her phone rang. She answered it. It was Haggerty.

"They're both in labor," Haggerty exclaimed excitedly. "Moonrise started last night. But it looks like having her friend in labor has kicked Mona Lisa into labor as well."

Louise checked her watch again. "I'll be there in about twenty to twenty-five minutes," she said, mentally calculating the distance from the compound, not from the clinic or her home. "I just need a few extra minutes to get dressed and get up there."

"Okay, hurry up."

She jumped into her clothes. When she turned around, she saw Rory coming out of the bathroom, putting on the same clothes as yesterday. She said, "You don't have to come. I know you're tired."

He never said a word. He walked to the bedroom door and opened it for her. She stepped out and said, "That was Haggerty. Both horses are in labor."

Again he didn't say a word as he nudged her toward the kitchen.

"We don't have time for breakfast," she protested.

Alfred heard that, and a frown crossed his face. "Only takes two seconds. Hold on." He raced into the kitchen and packed up something.

Bailey arrived with two coffee mugs. "Just bring them back," she said and stopped. "Are you going to the clinic?"

"No, I have two horses to watch over. The two I mentioned last night."

"Babies?" Bailey said with a big smile. "Let's hope all goes well."

Alfred hustled back out. He had a cloth-covered basket with him.

Rory lifted a corner, and a fresh croissant looked up at him. "You're a good man, Alfred."

"Just return the basket," Alfred scolded.

Louise walked outside and said, "The same truck? I really need to get my own vehicle again."

"The truck," he said.

She got in, put her travel mug of coffee in the holder and buckled up. By the time she was settled, Rory was out of the compound and onto the main road. "Are the horses in trouble?"

"It's hard to say. I'm hoping not. No need to expect trouble, I just know Haggerty's worried."

Rory nodded. "New fathers are always the worst."

She chuckled. "Haggerty's had lots of babies. But these horses hold a special spot in his heart."

With Rory driving, they made it to Haggerty's place in twenty-five minutes. Haggerty was overjoyed when he saw them. "Moonrise just had her baby. It's a colt," he said, dancing from foot to foot. "I haven't been in to see her. I'm trying to give her a moment."

Louise smiled. "That's good news. And Mom and baby need time together. I'll check her first."

When she got to the stall, Moonrise nickered at her. Louise stepped inside and gently patted the new mom. With tears in her eyes, she watched as the little one struggled to his feet. Within minutes, he had made it to a propped-up version with his legs splayed out, holding his body in a precariously balanced position. He was too adorable. From what she could see, he was perfectly healthy. She gave Moonrise a quick glance over, saw she was doing just fine, gave her a hug and a little bit of extra grain, and said, "She's doing great."

Haggerty opened the stall door and let her out.

"Where's Mona Lisa?" she asked.

He led her back to the biggest stall.

"She gets the grand room, does she?" Louise teased.

He blushed and shrugged. "You know how I feel about

this little lady."

Louise looked into the stall to see the mare standing and shaking; every few minutes a tremor would slide down her spine. She was definitely in labor. Louise ran her hand down the beautiful animal's neck.

Mona Lisa nickered gently in her throat.

"It's okay, sweetie. This is your first, and you have no idea what's going on." Louise checked her out and found the foal in the wrong position. She swore softly.

"What is it?" Haggerty called. "What's wrong?"

She sighed. "I've got four feet."

He stared at her. "Twins or a bad birth position?"

"I'll let you know in a few minutes. I need water," she said. She grabbed her medical bag, and, when Haggerty brought the water, she pulled her T-shirt sleeves up well over her shoulders, rolled them to keep them there, quickly washed up, lathering both entire arms, then raising them, and stepped behind the mare. She talked to her gently as she slowly eased one hand in, following the legs back up to the body. It took a few minutes to understand what was actually presenting itself. She grinned. With any luck, Haggerty was about to become a very happy man.

But first she had to shift the bodies so the twins weren't fighting to come out at the same time. That was a recipe for disaster. Determining which one was farther down the passage, she gently pushed the smaller of the two back up again. As soon as she did that, the first one, now no longer obstructed, slid free of the birth canal.

The magic of birth was a phenomenon that never failed to awe her. Mona Lisa turned to nicker at the young one. He still had the sack over his nose, and Louise quickly broke it open, letting his mom do the rest. But she knew the second baby was still to come, and new mothers weren't the best at handling twins. Louise would stay exactly where she was until that second one was born.

Ten minutes later Mom strained again. Talking quietly, Louise kept an eye on the baby's progress. When the hooves came back out again, this time the back two with a tail, she smiled. This would be a normal birth. As long as it was alive. When the second baby fell to the hay below, Louise was a little concerned because it wasn't moving much.

She ripped the sack from her face as Mona Lisa turned and nuzzled the body. The baby was struggling. Louise rubbed her chest to help clear the mucus from her lungs. When she then checked the baby's throat and pulled out a great big gob there and threw it to the straw, the filly breathed, her chest rising and falling. She was weaker than her brother and would need more care, but Louise could see the filly was healthy enough. Louise shifted the second one closer to the first, so Mom could look after both at the same time. As Louise watched, Mona Lisa stood gently over both, delighted with her two babies.

Louise stood and walked toward Haggerty. If there was ever a proud papa, it was him. He had tears in his eyes, and his face was wreathed in smiles. "Two of them," he whispered in awe. "Oh, my gosh, two of them."

She smiled, looked at herself, completely covered in muck and sighed. "We'll have to take that detour to my place and get a change of clothes," she said to Rory.

The gentlest look was on his face as he studied her. He nodded and said, "No problem. That was in the plan anyway."

She didn't want to leave the animals. There was something so special about being around newborns like this. She talked to Haggerty for a few minutes about their care. "I'll come back at the end of the day. Don't hesitate to call me if you are concerned. We need to make sure they're nursing. So …"

He shook his head. "I'm not leaving them. I'll be here all morning. We will make sure they are both eating."

She nodded. The colt was on his legs, trying hard to find Mom. Mona Lisa, being new and inexperienced, wasn't exactly sure what she could do.

"I'll stay a little longer to make sure they each get that first dose of colostrum," Louise said, walking back over to help. She nudged the little colt until his mouth attached to a teat. Instantly he started to work it.

She moved to the little filly trying to get up, but it was weaker. With a little assistance from Louise, the baby gained her feet and stood for a long moment, trying to find her balance. Mona Lisa gently nickered at her. Finally she stumbled to Mom's side and latched on for her first meal too. Satisfied that with a good dose of the colostrum from their first nursing, they'd both be just fine, Louise stepped away and said, "Okay, I'll leave it to you. I'll be back later today."

She looked at herself and smiled. "And everybody thinks being a vet is a glamorous job." She laughed a full-bodied freely loving-life laugh. Why not? It was a great day.

RORY EYED HER clothes. "It's a messy job, isn't it?"

She chuckled. "Sometimes, yes. I normally carry a towel in my vehicle and a change of clothes. But …" She looked at him sideways. "Remember that part about needing my vehicle again?"

At the truck, he pulled out an old towel from the back seat and handed it to her. She brushed off the best she could and said, "Let's just head to my place. I can get changed fast enough there."

He hopped in, and, with a friendly honk at Haggerty who was waving, they zipped down the long driveway and back to the main road. "That was quite the job," Rory said. "It's obvious you love your work."

"I love the animals," she said happily. "And this day is a hell of a lot better than it could have been."

He'd lived and worked on a ranch long enough to understand. He pulled up to her apartment and said, "Let's go. You've got barely enough time to make your first appointment at eight-thirty."

"We have a little bit longer than that. Because it's Saturday, my first appointment is at nine."

"Great. C'mon. Let's go then." He hopped out of the truck, waited for her. Within minutes they stood outside her apartment.

She took a deep breath, unlocked the door and followed Rory in. She remained at the entranceway while Rory checked out the whole apartment. Nothing appeared different. At his nod, she smiled happily and headed to the bedroom.

He paced, sending a text to Ice and to Logan, updating them on the morning. When Louise finally came back out, her skin shiny and pink, her hair was still in the same braid she had pleated it in earlier, but now she wore clean clothes. He smiled and said, "Ready for the day?"

"But maybe a good one. Mannford's sting netted several of the top men in the drug cartel. He's getting answers from one of them right now. It was a member of the cleaning company that killed their man in jail. So that's a start. Also one of the two original men that were killed at the clinic was the scout at your place. He screwed the security system so he could return later when the clinic was closed. He's also giving the details of where the drugs are being manufactured in Mexico and shipped across the border. So huge progress."

"It'll be another long one," she admitted. "But it is what it is."

With a last glance around, she stepped out of the apartment, and he locked up behind her and led her back to the truck. He opened the passenger door for her to get in. As soon as she buckled up, he shut the door and turned to walk around to the driver's side. That's when he was attacked. A vehicle peeled out of nowhere and drove so close to him he couldn't move. Another man raced around from the apartment and threw a hood over his head, and, with a hard punch, he went down. Just before he lost consciousness, he heard Louise scream at the top of her lungs for him.

And then the darkness took him.

When he opened his eyes again, he surveyed his surroundings, finding one large space, empty except for him and Louise. She was unconscious beside him, tied to a chair the same as he was. And of course his hat was missing. Damn, that was the third one in as many years. In a low voice he muttered, "Louise, can you hear me?"

She murmured something.

"Wake up. Wake up."

She shifted on the chair, slowly rolling her head toward him.

He hated to see her like that, but he knew they wouldn't be alone for long. He couldn't believe he had been taken just outside her apartment. Frustration and anger wouldn't help them now though. Only that's all he could think about. Then he remembered the text he'd just sent to the others, saying they were heading to the clinic. However, if anybody checked in at the clinic, how long would it take them to clue in something had happened? Had the kidnappers left any sign for Levi and the others to follow?

Rory doubted it. It would just look like they never left her apartment building. He tested his feet, but they were tied tight against his chair. His hands as well. He shifted them, looking for any kind of give. He had tools hidden in his boot heel if they were still there. But he had to get loose first. He had a double-jointed thumb, but it wasn't enough to get him out of his restraints this time. He checked Louise's restraints.

Her feet didn't appear to be tied quite as tightly. Neither did her hands. Men often thought women were incapable of getting out of anything. So they were treated easier. He was all for that. But he wasn't so sure about Louise. The bindings might be too tight for her to do anything. He kept working his hands, trying to figure out what he could use to get them free. The floor was cement, and the room had a single window at head height. The one and only door was on the same wall as the window. It appeared to be steel due to the rivets along its frame. They could be in a basement somewhere. That in itself was unusual. Not many places in Texas had basements. Or it could be a fabricating shop. As he considered that, it seemed more likely. He studied the floor, looking for anything he might use to get free. But there was nothing.

"Louise, wake up."

Her voice was low when she said, "I'm awake. I don't really want to be. But I'm awake."

"Test your bindings. See if you can get your hands

loose."

She straightened in her chair and winced. She struggled with her hands and shook her head.

"There are a couple tricks you can try." He slowly led her through some attempts to slide one hand out.

She struggled and swore and cursed until suddenly she turned and said, "My thumb is out."

He held his breath as she managed to slide out the rest of her fingers, and the rope dropped to the ground behind her. She bent to look at her feet. That was even easier. She took off her shoes, slipped her feet from the relatively loose ties and stood. She raced to his hands and struggled to untie the knots.

"Don't bother untying them. See if my phone is still is my pocket, then get the knife in my right boot heel." He lifted his hips and straightened out his thighs enough that she could get her hand inside his pocket. She shook her head, then dropped to his feet, as he walked her through the trick to twist apart his boot heel. She pulled out the penknife, popped open the blade and cut his ties. "See if they left your phone with you."

She checked her pockets and pulled out her phone.

On his feet, he took the knife from her and held it at his side. He motioned at the ropes. "Grab those. We'll need them."

She nodded, hurriedly collected them and stuffed them in her pockets as best as she could with the ends dangling out.

He walked to the window and peered out. There was a large parking lot, but he saw no vehicles. He saw no guards either, but they could be flattened against the building. "I don't know if they've gone, or there were no vehicles here to begin with." He motioned at the door and said, "When I go through there, it could get crazy real fast."

She looked at him and said, "We need to let the others know."

He nodded toward her phone, still in her hand. "Text Ice."

While she did that, he approached the door and placed an ear against it to see if he could hear anything. When there was nothing, he tried to turn the knob. It was locked. He pulled out a little tool kit from the back flap in the middle of his belt as he analyzed the screws holding the knob in place. Those he could handle. He unscrewed the ones that held the doorknob and managed to quietly slide the bolt out of the door. Motioning her to stay behind him, he slowly opened the door.

Bullets slammed into the room. He pulled back, his arm holding her safely behind him. He kept his arm pressed against her to hold her against him. Footsteps raced toward him. Sounded like a pair of guys. He waited. With his knife in hand, he knew the first thing through that door would be a weapon. As far as he was concerned, that weapon belonged to him.

Sure enough, seconds later, moving so slowly they were obviously prepared for an ambush, the nose of a gun appeared around the corner of the door. Rory grabbed the weapon, dropped to his knees, his fist shoving the first man's gun arm around, and Rory shot the second man. Rory didn't know if he'd killed him or not; he was too busy trying to subdue the man in his arms.

This one was more of a fighter.

Louise stepped out to face the man and kicked him hard in the balls. The man screamed and dropped to his knees.

Rory pinned him to the floor, lashing his hands together with a piece of rope from Louise. She handed him a second length of rope, and then he did the same to his feet.

He grabbed Louise's phone and sent a second text. **Two secured, one is injured. Still looking.**

He jumped to his feet, both weapons now in his hands. He looked at her, then held out a handgun for her. She grinned, accepting it. "Hell, yes. This is Texas. I really don't like to go into any trouble without a weapon of my own."

He flashed her a grin, loving her spunk along with everything else he'd learned about her. Keeping her behind him, he opened the door a bit more and peered through it to watch a vehicle pull up to the front with several men getting out.

The first one shouted and pointed. The others took one look at Rory and raised their weapons.

Rory fired. The windshield blew apart with his shot. He pulled back and slammed the steel door closed, hearing bullets slam into the outside. He had counted four men. He quickly texted the compound again. **One more down. Three more from a vehicle outside the building.**

He had barely hit Send before the window beside him shattered. He ducked underneath the frame and came up on the far side, lined up for a shot and took out a second man. A hail of bullets came his way. He looked around the room for another way to get more shots in. He had two more of those assholes to take out. With any luck, they would think he'd been shot, but he couldn't count on it.

So far it had been relatively easy, but he couldn't rely on that continuing. As he looked at Louise, he saw her ashen face and how she held her arm. He swore and raced to her side.

"It's nothing," she whispered. "Just glass."

He studied the wound, a razor-thin cut that was bleeding pretty heavily. He knew she would know how to take care of it—once again everybody had their specialties. He nodded, collected her weapon, then ran back to the window and peered out of the corner, saw two men with their weapons trained on the window and door. He couldn't open the door without being fired upon. What he needed was a chance to sneak up on them. He noted some kind of hoist raised up to the ceiling on the far side of the room. This place may have been used for vehicles at one time, maybe as a chop shop, but then in a warehouse-type setting, the hoist could've been for suspending other things.

He shoved one of the weapons in the front of his jeans and the other in the back. He jumped and caught the bottom part of the rope, pulled himself up onto the hoist. Moving as fast as he could, he maneuvered himself across the steel beam to where he could see one of the men outside. He popped off a shot and gave a knowing smile as his target dropped dead. They were down to one asshole.

The other man tucked in behind the car. Crouched low, his shots were all over the place as if he couldn't pinpoint where Rory was. That worked. He needed a chance to get this asshole. Just then he heard vehicles arriving behind the last gunman. Rory hoped they were aware of the shooter out there. Two trucks raced toward the shooter who started firing. From where he lay, Rory could see Logan lift a weapon, line it up and pull the trigger.

The man's head exploded backward against the trunk of the car.

Rory swung down, dropped himself to the cement floor. He raced over to Louise, sitting against the wall. "The cavalry came."

She smiled at him. "Nah," she said calmly. "The cavalry lives with me all the time." She stood and threw her good arm around his head, and he held her tight.

Chapter 14

S HE WAS BACK in the compound, even though she had protested how she was perfectly capable of going to the clinic. Instead they'd hauled her straight back here. Nancy had called in Jimmy to take her spot, giving the briefest of explanations. Now Alfred appeared to be in his element: fussing over her. Ice had cleaned the wound, determined it didn't need any stitches, but, because it would look ugly if it wasn't closed properly, she popped in a couple while Louise watched.

"You're very good at that."

Ice smiled. "I probably have more field experience than you have clinical experience."

Louise nodded. "Sometimes life is like that, isn't it?"

"You did good," Ice said. "Happy to have you on my team any day."

Louise smiled, feeling the warmth of friendship she hadn't expected. She hadn't really expected to find any of this actually. She'd spent the last five busy years building a business. After she had completed her education, it had seemed like a natural progression. But she hadn't imagined that progression to take every waking moment of her day. Between staffing issues and building new clients who came and went, she'd found herself working all the time.

Until she saw the camaraderie and friendships that had

formed at Levi's compound, she hadn't realized how much she wanted more of that in her life. And how much else she might have missed out on because she'd been so focused on work. As much as she wanted these people as friends, she didn't want them to look at her and always see a woman in need.

She said as much to Ice.

Ice looked at her in surprise and chuckled. "That'll never happen. We are a fully vibrant, dynamic unit. Everybody here has a place. We don't knock Bailey because she doesn't want to go out on a mission because her mission is in the kitchen, and we are all delighted to eat her efforts. Everybody here has a place, and everybody here revels in doing what it is they are good at. They have to learn a lot of things they aren't good at too," Ice said quietly. "It's part of living in a compound that has been under attack before. We all have alarm stations to go to. We all have things we do in emergency situations." She smiled, stood and said, "Don't worry about it. You'll fit in just fine."

Louise wasn't sure what that meant. But Rory stepped around the corner and smiled at her. "Ice said I could come in."

He held a wiggling puppy who, even though she was full of energy, was also fighting off sleep. It was the nature of a young animal. They played and played until they dropped. Louise wondered if it wasn't the nature of all the animals here. She reached out her arms for the puppy. As soon as the puppy was transferred to her, she dropped her head and just cuddled her.

"This is Rose," Rory said.

Louise raised an eyebrow. "It's probably not a good idea to name them."

"Too late," Rory said. "As far as I'm concerned, this gal's mine."

"Only if Levi lets you keep her, right?"

"Well, there are six of them. Michael wants one, and he's got his own place. Of course Flynn and Anna have their own place but don't need any more animals. Alfred is insisting on two. A couple of the guys who will live in the apartments want to have one. I highly suspect not one of these pups will leave this complex."

She shook her head. "Then we better get them fixed and fast."

He chuckled. "Exactly."

She handed the big-bellied Rose back to Rory and said, "Interesting that you chose her."

"Oh, why?" Rory asked. "I'm not sure I chose her as much as she chose me."

"That's the thing, isn't it? I was there that day you arrived. She's the one that waddled over to you as if she already knew you would be a sucker for her."

He gently cuddled the sleeping pup in his arms and said, "I didn't realize how prophetic that day would be. But now that I look back on it …"

She hopped off the gurney. Even though Ice had given her some topical anesthetic, her arm was stinging pretty good. She focused on him and tried to keep any evidence of pain from registering on her face. She tilted her head at him and raised her eyebrows.

"Because that's also the same day I met you," Rory said. "I didn't understand Levi's words at the time. He said something to me after you left about me fitting right in, and I might as well just get used to it. And I've come to realize what he meant."

She stopped and stared at him, now with a frown crinkling her forehead. "Explain?"

"Everybody here is paired up. Everybody here has met somebody very special in their life, most of them while they were working at the compound. I didn't understand that's what he meant at the time, but I do now. Because he's right. I do fit in. And he's right in another way. I will get used to it."

Suspicious now, she narrowed her gaze and said, "What's *it?*"

"Having you in my life," he said quietly. "Having a relationship with you and seeing where it goes. Seeing if we can find the same magic everybody else here has already found."

She smiled, the corner of her lips tilting up. She hadn't dared hope he would have the same kind of feelings she had. That he appeared to was almost beyond belief. She felt truly blessed. "What's that smile for?" he asked. "You know, when a guy starts talking about his feelings, you are supposed to at least reassure him or give him the cold shoulder, so he knows where he stands."

She chuckled. "I'm glad you finally told me where you stand."

"Hey, that's not fair," he protested. "You haven't told me yet where you stand."

She shook her head and wrapped her good arm around him. "Sure I did, when I invited you into my shower last night."

"But that wasn't ..." and then he stopped and said, "Oh, that's why it took five years."

She nodded. "Exactly. I don't love lightly. But, when I do love, I love deep."

With Rose tucked into his arm, he closed the other one

around Louise and held her close. "In that case I'm doubly blessed."

She whispered against his heart, "And so am I."

Epilogue

BRANDON HORTON WASN'T sure what to make of Legendary Security. He'd been here two days, and so many people had been coming and going, it was hard to keep track of who was who. And then there were the puppies. Six of them. Although several were going to individual apartments on the property when they were old enough. But all the homes were connected to the men here.

Brandon only really felt comfortable in a chair propped up against the back wall out of the way. The trouble was, they weren't letting him stay there. Then Michael, and Rory sporting his new cowboy hat, had stuck close to not make him feel isolated.

Ice had walked over several times to get him to fill out paperwork. He'd done that and had passed it back and then continued to stay quiet in the background. He was getting paid, but he sure as hell didn't know why or what for. He'd expected to be shipped out on a job immediately, but so far that hadn't happened.

The phone rang in the house. He wasn't even sure who was supposed to answer it. He knew it wasn't him. He barely knew what was going on from day to day.

When Ice walked in, her tone clipped and urgent, the atmosphere shifted. Something was up. She turned on the big screen in the kitchen and hit an alarm on the side of the door. People poured into the room. He pulled farther back, watching curiously.

An image filled the screen.

"Kasha, you're on the screen. Go ahead."

"Ice, Bullard has gone missing," said a tall, lean young woman with long black hair, worry creasing her face and fatigue pulling on her features. "Six days ago, five of us traveled to his new property on the Tunisian border. He said he wanted to stay for another day alone. Get a feel for it. So he sent us away. We expected him back the next day, but when the pilot landed to pick him up, there was no sign of him. He hasn't answered his comm. Our men are out on multiple missions, so we're shorthanded here."

"We'll send four men. Two from here but Merk and Stone are in Europe. They'll arrive within a few hours of each other."

Brandon watched the relief light up Kasha's eyes. With her long dark hair and slightly honey-toned skin, she was a knockout. He could see some of the room behind her. It looked like the command center of a big military operation. He'd never seen anything like it in a personal home.

"How long?" Kasha asked in clipped tones.

Ice looked at her watch as if mentally calculating and said, "Twelve hours for the first pair. Faster if I can."

Kasha looked like she wanted to argue, then conceded quietly.

"In the meantime," Ice said, "gather as much information as you can. Who saw him last? Where? Did he have plans to go anywhere? What is his weapons situation like? Understand?"

"Understood." Kasha clicked something in front of her, and the screen went dark.

Levi stepped up beside Ice, their two heads bent in conversation.

Brandon watched the others explain about Bullard to those who weren't in the know. He actually knew Bullard, had met him a couple times. Not Kasha. He'd have remembered her.

Ice walked out of the room, Levi behind her. Brandon grabbed another cup of coffee and watched to see what, if anything, would come of this. After another hour, he headed to his room.

Levi caught up with him in the hallway. "Brandon, in three hours, you're leaving for the airport."

"Where am I going?" he asked, interested to see what his future with the company would hold. He'd been afraid he'd be stuck babysitting stars in California.

"Africa to find Bullard. And the time frame is *yesterday*."

And just like that Levi was gone.

This concludes Book 13 of Heroes for Hire: Rory's Rose.

Read about Brandon's Bliss: Heroes for Hire, Book 14

Heroes for Hire: Brandon's Bliss (Book #14)

Brandon, the newest member of Levi's team at Legendary Securities, heads to Africa. Bullard purchased a new holding there, but, shortly after arriving, went missing.

Kasha has worked for Bullard for five years. She's familiar with most of those who work for Legendary as well. Brandon proves his worth almost immediately, planning her boss's rescue and staying right by her side in the days that follow while they determine what imbroglio Bullard's stepped into. Accident or a deal gone horribly wrong, it seems Bullard was running guns and now his newest holding is under attack.

Their emotions, heightened by danger, run hot as Brandon positions himself instinctively at Kasha's side—which is exactly where he hopes to be permanently if they can just find a way out of this rapidly escalating mess.

Book 14 is available now!
To find out more visit Dale Mayer's website.
https://geni.us/DMBrandonUniversal

Other Military Series by Dale Mayer

SEALs of Honor

Heroes for Hire

SEALs of Steel

The K9 Files

The Mavericks

Bullards Battle

Hathaway House

Terkel's Team

Ryland's Reach: Bullard's Battle (Book #1)

Welcome to a new stand-alone but interconnected series from Dale Mayer. This is Bullard's story—and that of his team's. All raw, rough, incredibly capable men who have one goal: to find out who was behind the attack on their leader, before the attacker, or attackers, return to finish the job.

Stay tuned for more nonstop action as the men narrow down their suspects … and find a way to let love back into their own empty lives.

His rescue from the ocean after a horrible plane explosion was his top priority, in any way, shape, or form. A small sailboat and a nurse to do the job was more than Ryland hoped for.

When Tabi somehow drags him and his buddy Garret onboard and surprisingly gets them to a naval ship close by, Ryland figures he'd used up all his luck and his friend's too. Sure enough, those who attacked the plane they were in weren't content to let him slowly die in the ocean. No. Surviving had made him a target all over again.

Tabi isn't expecting her sailing holiday to include the rescue of two badly injured men and then to end with the loss of her beloved sailboat. Her instincts save them, but now she finds it tough to let them go—even as more of Bullard's team members come to them—until it becomes apparent that not only are Bullard and his men still targets ... but she is too.

BULLARD CHECKED THAT the helicopter was loaded with their bags and that his men were ready to leave.

He walked back one more time, his gaze on Ice. She'd never looked happier, never looked more perfect. His heart ached, but he knew she remained a caring friend and always would be. He opened his arms; she ran into them, and he held her close, whispering, "The offer still stands."

She leaned back and smiled up at him. "Maybe if and when Levi's been gone for a long enough time for me to forget," she said in all seriousness.

"That's not happening. You two, now three, will live long and happy lives together," he said, smiling down at the woman knew to be the most beautiful, inside and out. She would never be his, but he always kept a little corner of his heart open and available, in case she wanted to surprise him and to slide inside.

And then he realized she'd already been a part of his heart all this time. That was a good ten to fifteen years by now. But she kept herself in the friend category, and he understood because she and Levi, partners and now parents, were perfect together.

Bullard reached out and shook Levi's hand. "It was a hell of a blast," he said. "When you guys do a big splash, you really do a *big* splash."

Ice laughed. "A few days at home sounds perfect for me now."

"It looks great," he said, his hands on his hips as he surveyed the people in the massive pool surrounded by the palm trees, all designed and decked out by Ice. Right beside all the war machines that he heartily approved of. He grinned at her. "When are you coming over to visit?" His gaze went to Levi, raising his eyebrows back at her. "You guys should come over for a week or two or three."

"It's not a bad idea," Levi said. "We could use a long holiday, just not yet."

"That sounds familiar." Bullard grinned. "Anyway, I'm off. We'll hit the airport and then pick up the plane and head home." He added, "As always, call if you need me."

Everybody raised a hand as he returned to the helicopter and his buddy who was flying him to the airport. Ice had volunteered to shuttle him there, but he hadn't wanted to take her away from her family or to prolong the goodbye. He hopped inside, waving at everybody as the helicopter lifted. Two of his men, Ryland and Garret, were in the back seats. They always traveled with him.

Bullard would pick up the rest of his men in Australia. He stared down at the compound as he flew overhead. He preferred his compound at home, but damn they'd done a nice job here.

With everybody on the ground screaming goodbye, Bullard sailed over Houston, heading toward the airport. His two men never said a word. They all knew how he felt about Ice. But not one of them would cross that line and say anything. At least not if they expected to still have jobs.

It was one thing to fall in love with another man's woman, but another thing to fall in love with a woman who was so unique, so different, and so absolutely perfect that you knew, just knew, there was no hope of finding anybody else like her. But she and Levi had been together way before Bullard had ever met her, which made it that much more heartbreaking.

Still, he'd turned and looked forward. He had a full roster of jobs himself to focus on when he got home. Part of him was tired of the life; another part of him couldn't wait to head out on the next adventure. He managed to run everything from his command centers in one or two of his locations. He'd spent a lot of time and effort at the second one and kept a full team at both locations, yet preferred to spend most of his time at the old one. It felt more like home to him, and he'd like to be there now, but still had many more days before that could happen.

The helicopter lowered to the tarmac, he stepped out, said his goodbyes and walked across to where his private plane waited. It was one of the things that he loved, being a pilot of both helicopters and airplanes, and owning both birds himself.

That again was another way he and Ice were part of the same team, of the same mind-set. He'd been looking for another woman like Ice for himself, but no such luck. Sure, lots were around for short-term relationships, but most of them couldn't handle his lifestyle or the violence of the world that he lived in. He understood that.

The ones who did had a hard edge to them that he found difficult to live with. Bullard appreciated everybody's being alert and aware, but if there wasn't some softness in the women, they seemed to turn cold all the way through.

As he boarded his small plane, Ryland and Garret following behind, Bullard called out in his loud voice, "Let's go, slow pokes. We've got a long flight ahead of us."

The men grinned, confident Bullard was teasing, as was his usual routine during their off-hours.

"Well, we're ready, not sure about you though ..." Ryland said, smirking.

"We're waiting on you this time," Garret added with a chuckle. "Good thing you're the boss."

Bullard grinned at his two right-hand men. "Isn't that the truth?" He dropped his bags at one of the guys' feet and said, "Stow all this stuff, will you? I want to get our flight path cleared and get the hell out of here."

They'd all enjoyed the break. He tried to get over once a year to visit Ice and Levi and same in reverse. But it was time to get back to business. He started up the engines, got confirmation from the tower. They were heading to Australia for this next job. He really wanted to go straight back to Africa, but it would be a while yet. They'd refuel in Honolulu.

Ryland came in and sat down in the copilot's spot, buckled in, then asked, "You ready?"

Bullard laughed. "When have you ever known me *not* to be ready?" At that, he taxied down the runway. Before long he was up in the air, at cruising level, and heading to Hawaii. "Gotta love these views from up here," Bullard said. "This place is magical."

"It is once you get up above all the smog," he said. "Why Australia again?"

"Remember how we were supposed to check out that newest compound in Australia that I've had my eye on? Besides the alpha team is coming off that ugly job in Sydney. We'll give them a day or two of R&R then head home."

"Right. We could have some equally ugly payback on that job."

Bullard shrugged. "That goes for most of our jobs. It's the life."

"And don't you have enough compounds to look after?"

"Yes I do, but that kid in me still looks to take over the world. Just remember that."

"Better you go home to Africa and look after your first two compounds," Ryland said.

"Maybe," Bullard admitted. "But it seems hard to not continue expanding."

"You need a partner," Ryland said abruptly. "That might ease the savage beast inside. Keep you home more."

"Well, the only one I like," he said, "is married to my best friend."

"I'm sorry about that," Ryland said quietly. "What a shit deal."

"No," Bullard said. "I came on the scene last. They were always meant to be together. Especially now they are a family."

"If you say so," Ryland said.

Bullard nodded. "Damn right, I say so."

And that set the tone for the next many hours. They landed in Hawaii, and while they fueled up everybody got off to stretch their legs by walking around outside a bit as this was a small private airstrip, not exactly full of hangars and tourists. Then they hopped back on board again for takeoff.

"I can fly," Ryland offered as they took off.

"We'll switch in a bit," Bullard said. "Surprisingly, I'm doing okay yet, but I'll let you take her down."

"Yeah, it's still a long flight," Ryland said studying the islands below. It was a stunning view of the area.

"I love the islands here. Sometimes I just wonder about the benefit of, you know, crashing into the sea, coming up on a deserted island, and finding the simple life again," Bullard said with a laugh.

"I hear you," Ryland said. "Every once in a while, I wonder the same."

Several hours later Ryland looked up and said abruptly, "We've made good time considering we've already passed Fiji."

Bullard yawned.

"Let's switch."

Bullard smiled, nodded, and said, "Fine. I'll hand it over to you."

Just then a funny noise came from the engine on the right side.

They looked at each other, and Ryland said, "Uh-oh. That's not good news."

Boom!

And the plane exploded.

Find Bullard's Battle (Book #1) here!

To find out more visit Dale Mayer's website.

https://geni.us/DMRylandUniversal

Damon's Deal: Terkel's Team (Book #1)

Welcome to a brand-new connected series of intrigue, betrayal, and ... murder, from the *USA Today* best-selling author Dale Mayer. A series with all the elements you've come to love, plus so much more… including psychics!

A betrayal from within has Terkel frantic to protect those he can, as his team falls one by one, from a murderous killer he helped create.

ICE POURED HERSELF a coffee and sat down at the compound's massive dining room table with the others. When her phone rang, she smiled at the number displayed. "Hey, Terk. How're you doing?" She put the call on Speakerphone.

"I'm okay," Terkel said, his voice distracted and tight.

"Terk?" Merk called from across the table. He got up and walked closer and sat across from Levi. "You don't sound too good, brother. What's up?"

"I'm fine," Terk said. "Or I will be. Right now, things are blown to shit."

"As in literally?" Merk asked.

"The entire group," Terk said, "they're all gone. I had a solid team of eight, and they're all gone."

"Dead?"

Several others stood to join them, gathered around Ice's phone. Levi stepped forward, his hand on Ice's shoulder. "Terk? Are they all dead?"

"No." Terk took a deep breath. "I'm not making sense. I'm sorry."

"Take it easy," Ice said, her voice calm and reassuring. "What do you mean, *they're all gone?*"

"All their abilities are gone," he said. "Something's happened to them. Somebody has deliberately removed whatever super senses they could utilize—or what we have been utilizing for the last ten years for the government." His tone was bitter. "When the US gov recently closed us down, they promised that our black ops department would never rise again, but I didn't expect them to attack us personally."

"What are you talking about?" Merk said in alarm, standing up now to stare at Ice's phone. "Are you in danger?"

"Maybe? I don't know," Terk said. "I need to find out exactly what the hell's going on."

"What can we do to help?" Ice asked.

Terk gave a broken laugh. "That's not why I'm calling. Well, it is, but it isn't."

Ice looked at Merk, who frowned, as he shook his head. Ice knew he and the others had heard Terk's stressed out tone and the completely confusing bits and pieces coming from his mouth. Ice said, "Terk, you're not making sense again. Take a breath and explain. Please. You're scaring me."

Terk took a long slow deep breath. "Tell Stone to open the gate," he said. "She's out there."

"Who's out there?" Levi asked, hopped up, looked outside, and shrugged.

"She's coming up the road now. You have to let her in."

"Who? Why?"

"*Because*," he said, "she's also harnessed with C-4."

"Jesus," Levi said, bolting to display the camera feeds to the big screen in the room. "Is it live?"

"It is, and she's been sent to you."

"Well, that's an interesting move," Ice said, her voice sharp, activating her comm to connect to Stone in the control room. "Who's after us?"

"I think it's rebels within the Iranian government. But it could be our own government. I don't know anymore," Terk snapped. "I also don't know how they got her so close to you. Or how they pinned your connection to me," he said. "I've been very careful."

"We can look after ourselves," Ice said immediately. "But who is this woman to you?"

"She's pregnant," he said, "so that adds to the intensity here."

"Understood. So who is the father? Is he connected somehow?"

There was silence on the other end.

Merk said, "Terk, talk to us."

"She's carrying my baby," Terk replied, his voice heavy.

Merk, his expression grim, looked at Ice, her face mirroring his shock. He asked, "How do you know her, Terk?"

"Brother, you don't understand," Terk said. "I've never met this woman before in my life." And, with that, the phone went dead.

Find Terkel's Team (Book #1) here!

To find out more visit Dale Mayer's website.

https://geni.us/DMTTDamonUniversal

Author's Note

Thank you for reading Rory's Rose: Heroes for Hire, Book 13! If you enjoyed the book, please take a moment and leave a short review.

Dear reader,

I love to hear from readers, and you can contact me at my website: www.dalemayer.com or at my Facebook author page. To be informed of new releases and special offers, sign up for my newsletter or follow me on BookBub. And if you are interested in joining Dale Mayer's Reader Group, here is the Facebook sign up page. http://geni.us/DaleMayerFBGroup

Cheers,
Dale Mayer

About the Author

Dale Mayer is a *USA Today* best-selling author, best known for her SEALs military romances, her Psychic Visions series, and her Lovely Lethal Garden cozy series. Her contemporary romances are raw and full of passion and emotion (Broken But … Mending, Hathaway House series). Her thrillers will keep you guessing (Kate Morgan, By Death series), and her romantic comedies will keep you giggling (*It's a Dog's Life*, a stand-alone novella; and the Broken Protocols series, starring Charming Marvin, the cat).

Dale honors the stories that come to her—and some of them are crazy, break all the rules and cross multiple genres!

To go with her fiction, she also writes nonfiction in many different fields, with books available on résumé writing, companion gardening, and the US mortgage system. All her books are available in print and ebook format.

Connect with Dale Mayer Online

Dale's Website – www.dalemayer.com
Twitter – @DaleMayer
Facebook Page – geni.us/DaleMayerFBFanPage
Facebook Group – geni.us/DaleMayerFBGroup
BookBub – geni.us/DaleMayerBookbub
Instagram – geni.us/DaleMayerInstagram
Goodreads – geni.us/DaleMayerGoodreads
Newsletter – geni.us/DaleNews

Also by Dale Mayer

Published Adult Books:

Bullard's Battle
Ryland's Reach, Book 1
Cain's Cross, Book 2
Eton's Escape, Book 3
Garret's Gambit, Book 4
Kano's Keep, Book 5
Fallon's Flaw, Book 6
Quinn's Quest, Book 7
Bullard's Beauty, Book 8
Bullard's Best, Book 9

Terkel's Team
Damon's Deal, Book 1

Kate Morgan
Simon Says… Hide, Book 1

Hathaway House
Aaron, Book 1
Brock, Book 2
Cole, Book 3
Denton, Book 4

Elliot, Book 5

Finn, Book 6

Gregory, Book 7

Heath, Book 8

Iain, Book 9

Jaden, Book 10

Keith, Book 11

Lance, Book 12

Melissa, Book 13

Nash, Book 14

Owen, Book 15

Hathaway House, Books 1–3

Hathaway House, Books 4–6

Hathaway House, Books 7–9

The K9 Files

Ethan, Book 1

Pierce, Book 2

Zane, Book 3

Blaze, Book 4

Lucas, Book 5

Parker, Book 6

Carter, Book 7

Weston, Book 8

Greyson, Book 9

Rowan, Book 10

Caleb, Book 11

Kurt, Book 12

Tucker, Book 13

Harley, Book 14

The K9 Files, Books 1–2

The K9 Files, Books 3–4

The K9 Files, Books 5–6

The K9 Files, Books 7–8

The K9 Files, Books 9–10

The K9 Files, Books 11–12

Lovely Lethal Gardens

Arsenic in the Azaleas, Book 1

Bones in the Begonias, Book 2

Corpse in the Carnations, Book 3

Daggers in the Dahlias, Book 4

Evidence in the Echinacea, Book 5

Footprints in the Ferns, Book 6

Gun in the Gardenias, Book 7

Handcuffs in the Heather, Book 8

Ice Pick in the Ivy, Book 9

Jewels in the Juniper, Book 10

Killer in the Kiwis, Book 11

Lifeless in the Lilies, Book 12

Murder in the Marigolds, Book 13

Lovely Lethal Gardens, Books 1–2

Lovely Lethal Gardens, Books 3–4

Lovely Lethal Gardens, Books 5–6

Lovely Lethal Gardens, Books 7–8

Lovely Lethal Gardens, Books 9–10

Psychic Vision Series

Tuesday's Child

Hide 'n Go Seek

Maddy's Floor

Garden of Sorrow

Knock Knock...

Rare Find

Eyes to the Soul

Now You See Her

Shattered

Into the Abyss

Seeds of Malice

Eye of the Falcon

Itsy-Bitsy Spider

Unmasked

Deep Beneath

From the Ashes

Stroke of Death

Ice Maiden

Snap, Crackle...

Psychic Visions Books 1–3

Psychic Visions Books 4–6

Psychic Visions Books 7–9

By Death Series

Touched by Death

Haunted by Death

Chilled by Death

By Death Books 1–3

Broken Protocols – Romantic Comedy Series
Cat's Meow
Cat's Pajamas
Cat's Cradle
Cat's Claus
Broken Protocols 1-4

Broken and... Mending
Skin
Scars
Scales (of Justice)
Broken but... Mending 1-3

Glory
Genesis
Tori
Celeste
Glory Trilogy

Biker Blues
Morgan: Biker Blues, Volume 1
Cash: Biker Blues, Volume 2

SEALs of Honor
Mason: SEALs of Honor, Book 1
Hawk: SEALs of Honor, Book 2
Dane: SEALs of Honor, Book 3
Swede: SEALs of Honor, Book 4
Shadow: SEALs of Honor, Book 5
Cooper: SEALs of Honor, Book 6

Heroes for Hire

Levi's Legend: Heroes for Hire, Book 1

Stone's Surrender: Heroes for Hire, Book 2

Merk's Mistake: Heroes for Hire, Book 3

Rhodes's Reward: Heroes for Hire, Book 4

Flynn's Firecracker: Heroes for Hire, Book 5

Logan's Light: Heroes for Hire, Book 6

Harrison's Heart: Heroes for Hire, Book 7

Saul's Sweetheart: Heroes for Hire, Book 8

Dakota's Delight: Heroes for Hire, Book 9

Tyson's Treasure: Heroes for Hire, Book 10

Jace's Jewel: Heroes for Hire, Book 11

Rory's Rose: Heroes for Hire, Book 12

Brandon's Bliss: Heroes for Hire, Book 13

Liam's Lily: Heroes for Hire, Book 14

North's Nikki: Heroes for Hire, Book 15

Anders's Angel: Heroes for Hire, Book 16

Reyes's Raina: Heroes for Hire, Book 17

Dezi's Diamond: Heroes for Hire, Book 18

Vince's Vixen: Heroes for Hire, Book 19

Ice's Icing: Heroes for Hire, Book 20

Julian's Joy: Heroes for Hire, Book 21

Galen's Gemma: Heroes for Hire, Book 22

Zack's Zest: Heroes for Hire, Book 23

Bonaparte's Belle: Heroes for Hire, Book 24

Heroes for Hire, Books 1–3

Heroes for Hire, Books 4–6

Heroes for Hire, Books 7–9

Diesel, Book 13

Jerricho, Book 14

The Mavericks, Books 1–2

The Mavericks, Books 3–4

The Mavericks, Books 5–6

The Mavericks, Books 7–8

The Mavericks, Books 9–10

The Mavericks, Books 11–12

Collections

Dare to Be You…

Dare to Love…

Dare to be Strong…

RomanceX3

Standalone Novellas

It's a Dog's Life

Riana's Revenge

Second Chances

Published Young Adult Books:

Family Blood Ties Series

Vampire in Denial

Vampire in Distress

Vampire in Design

Vampire in Deceit

Vampire in Defiance

Vampire in Conflict

Vampire in Chaos

Vampire in Crisis
Vampire in Control
Vampire in Charge
Family Blood Ties Set 1–3
Family Blood Ties Set 1–5
Family Blood Ties Set 4–6
Family Blood Ties Set 7–9
Sian's Solution, A Family Blood Ties Series Prequel
Novelette

Design series
Dangerous Designs
Deadly Designs
Darkest Designs
Design Series Trilogy

Standalone
In Cassie's Corner
Gem Stone (a Gemma Stone Mystery)
Time Thieves

Published Non-Fiction Books:

Career Essentials
Career Essentials: The Résumé
Career Essentials: The Cover Letter
Career Essentials: The Interview
Career Essentials: 3 in 1

www.ingramcontent.com/pod-product-compliance
Lightning Source LLC
Chambersburg PA
CBHW071523110726
47908CB00003B/929